"Welcome, Ms. Tyler, to Summerhill." Scott Galbraith's mouth twisted in a sardonic smile.

"Yesterday, as I recall, you pronounced my children the worst-behaved you had ever seen," he continued. With an exaggeratedly courtly gesture he invited her to come inside. "From now on they are in your hands."

As Willow walked past him, her heart hammering like mad, he added, "I should warn you that in the last twenty months my children have gone through no less than five top-notch nannies."

"I wonder," Scott continued in that already so familiar brown velvet voice, "just how long *you* are going to last."

Grace Green grew up in Scotland, but later immigrated to Canada with her husband and children. They settled in "Beautiful Super Natural B.C.," and Grace now lives in a house just minutes from ocean, beaches, mountains and rain forest. She makes no secret of her favorite occupation—her bumper sticker reads, I'd Rather Be Writing Romance! Grace also enjoys walking the seawall, gardening, getting together with other authors…and watching her characters come to life, because she knows that once they do, they will take over and write her stories for her.

Books by Grace Green

HARLEQUIN ROMANCE®
3706—THE NANNY'S SECRET
3714—THE PREGNANCY PLAN
3737—FOREVER WIFE AND MOTHER

Don't miss any of our special offers. Write to us at the following address for information on our newest releases.

Harlequin Reader Service
U.S.: 3010 Walden Ave., P.O. Box 1325, Buffalo, NY 14269
Canadian: P.O. Box 609, Fort Erie, Ont. L2A 5X3

HIS POTENTIAL WIFE
Grace Green

HARLEQUIN®

TORONTO • NEW YORK • LONDON
AMSTERDAM • PARIS • SYDNEY • HAMBURG
STOCKHOLM • ATHENS • TOKYO • MILAN • MADRID
PRAGUE • WARSAW • BUDAPEST • AUCKLAND

ISBN 0-373-03781-3

HIS POTENTIAL WIFE

First North American Publication 2004.

Copyright © 2001 by Grace Green.

This edition published by arrangement with Harlequin Books S.A.

® and TM are trademarks of the publisher. Trademarks indicated with
® are registered in the United States Patent and Trademark Office, the
Canadian Trade Marks Office and in other countries.

Visit us at www.eHarlequin.com

Printed in U.S.A.

CHAPTER ONE

"WHAT I want, Mrs. Trent, is a plain-Jane nanny."

"A...*plain-Jane* nanny, Dr. Galbraith?" Ida Trent looked startled. "I'm not sure I underst—"

Scott Galbraith shot forward in his chair. "Mikey, get your fingers out of there!" He swept his son onto his lap a nanosecond before the two-year-old managed to tug a purple African violet from its clay pot on Ida Trent's tidy desk.

The owner of the Trent Employment Agency cleared her throat. "Dr. Galbraith, I'm not sure exactly what you—"

"Let me spell it out." Abstractedly Scott dusted potting soil from Mikey's fingers. "I want a woman whose top priority—in fact, her only priority!—is caring for my three motherless children. I want a woman who doesn't dream of orange blossom or see me as a potential husband—"

He broke off as four-year-old Amy stomped toward the office door. "Amy, get back here!"

Amy plodded on.

"Lizzie!" Urgently he prodded his elder daughter, who was slouched, reading, against the end of the desk. "Would you please catch your sister before she hits the street!"

Lizzie sighed as only a put-upon eight-year-old can sigh and took off to restrain her sister. Then none-too-gently she pushed the sturdy redhead down onto a sofa

5

by the window. "Stay there," she snapped. "And try not to be such an absolute *pest!*"

Amy's blue eyes puddled with tears. "I am *not* a pest!"

"Are, too!"

"Am not!"

Lizzie flicked back her long blond braid and curled her upper lip in a sneer. *"Pest, pest, pest!"* Stalking back to the end of the desk, she resumed her slouching position and fixed her gaze again on the pages of her book.

Scott opened his mouth to chastise her...but closed it again when he noticed that his daughter's face had become paper-white and her lips were trembling.

The sight reduced him to despair and helplessness— emotions that had become all too familiar to him over the past twenty months. He felt his heart go out to Lizzie, aware that her emotions must often be in a turmoil similar to his own. Of the three children, she was the one who missed her mother most. And he knew that because she was the eldest, he'd often stuck her with too much responsibility. So instead of berating her, he returned his attention to the woman seated across the desk from him.

"Now, Mrs. Trent, where were we?"

"You were telling me you wanted a plain-Jane nanny—"

"And one who isn't man mad!"

"—and one who isn't man mad. Actually—" Ida Trent looked thoughtful "—I believe I have someone who will suit you perfectly. She has *excellent* references and a true love of children...and I know, for a fact, that the last thing she's looking for in her life is romance.

Fortunately she's between positions and could start right away.''

An ominous warm dampness suddenly seeped from Mikey's diaper-padded bottom through the fabric of Scott's brand-new designer pants. Oh, great. Just what he needed.

"So tell me," he said resignedly, "does this paragon of virtue have a name?"

"She does, Dr. Galbraith. Her name is Willow Tyler.''

"Hey, Mom!"

Willow Tyler glanced up from her sunny bench and as she saw her son race toward her from the Rec Center's entrance, she stuffed her wallet back into her handbag.

She would worry about her low bank balance later. For the present she would focus on Jamie. Once she got another job—and she prayed that would happen soon— she'd have little enough time to spend with him.

She couldn't help smiling now as he approached her, his black hair dripping wet, his T-shirt outside-in, his sneakers ineptly tied. She itched to tidy him...but he was the most independent child on the face of the earth and she knew he would balk. From the beginning, he'd adamantly refused to let her tend to him after his swimming lessons.

"You're not allowed into the men's changing rooms," he'd announced. "And—sorry, Mom!—no *way* am I going into the ladies' changing rooms!"

Now—reeking of chlorine—he danced in front of her, his gray-green eyes eager. "Can we go to Morganti's for a burger? Please? I'm *starving!*"

Willow hesitated. She hated spending money on fast

food…yet she hated to disappoint Jamie; he didn't ask for much. "All right—but let's not make a habit of it."

Morganti's was only a hop and a skip away, at the corner of Fifth Avenue and Fir Street. When they got inside, Jamie said, "Are you having a burger, too, Mom?"

"No, I'll have a hot caramel sundae."

"I'll get it."

He'd adopted a take-charge tone and she knew that for the moment, he'd assumed his man-of-the-house role. He held out his hand for money. "You want nuts on it?"

"No nuts." She gave him a ten-dollar bill. "But I'll have double caramel."

"Can I have a large cola?"

"Sure."

"Yes!" Gleefully he thrust his backpack at her and scampered off to take his place at the counter.

Willow sat at a vacant table and tucked his backpack under her chair before glancing around.

The restaurant was busy but Tradition, British Columbia, was a small town and she knew most of the people there. With a friendly wave she acknowledged those who sent a smile her way.

At the next table was a group of four—a man and three small children. He was dark-haired and broad-shouldered but he had his back to her so she couldn't see his face. She had a plain view of the children, though, and they were strangers to her—a lovely blond girl of around nine, who was reading while eating a burger; a younger redheaded girl with grubby tear-stained cheeks; and a little boy in a high chair, whose fair hair was smeared with what looked like ketchup from the French fries spread out on his tray.

The man got up and she heard him say in a deep voice that made her think of dark brown velvet, "Lizzie, keep an eye on these two. I'm going for a coffee refill."

He strode away toward the counter and she saw that he was quite tall, and wearing a beautifully cut charcoal-gray suit. She also noticed that he walked in an athletic way that spoke of lean muscles and coiled strength, and with a sense of purpose that gave an impression of self-confidence.

He took up his place in one of the short lineups and as he did, she saw Jamie turn from the counter.

He began walking toward her, carefully balancing his tray. She held her breath as the tall cola cup wavered, but he paused and it steadied and he resumed his precarious journey.

All went well until a fracas suddenly erupted at the next table. The tot in the high chair let out an enraged howl: apparently the middle child had stolen a handful of French fries from his tray because the one called Lizzie snapped, "Put those back, Amy! You said you didn't want any fries. When are you going to stop being such a *pest!*" She grabbed Amy's fist and tore the half-dozen fries from her.

"Give those back!" screamed Amy and reached after them.

"No way, you little pest! Pest! Pest! Pest!" Taunting her sister, Lizzie swung her hand away, out into the aisle...

And banged it into Jamie's carefully balanced tray, knocking it wildly from his hands.

For a split second, silence fell on the group of three. The boy's mouth froze in a wide-open O; the redhead's screams stopped as if chopped off by an ax; and the girl called Lizzie's expression turned to one of stark shock.

And then…oh, the clatter as the tray bounced on the tiled floor; the mess as the cola spilled out in a sticky stream; the cry of dismay from Jamie as he stared in horror at the demise of his gleefully anticipated treat.

But even as Willow shot to her feet, the three children resumed their squabbling.

"That was all your fault, Amy. If you hadn't been such a pest—"

"You did it!" Amy's shout was outraged. "It was—"

"I want more fries!" The little boy hammered his hands on his tray. "More, more, more!"

Jamie was quietly sobbing.

"Oh, honey!" Willow hunkered down and gathered his slight body to her. "Don't cry. It wasn't your fault, you were being so very careful. We'll get someone to clean up this mess, and then we'll just order the same thing again."

He leaned away from her and furiously swiped his hands over his teary eyes. "I want to go home. I don't like it in here today." He glared at the still-squabbling trio who were paying him no attention. "And I don't like *them!* They didn't even say they were sorry—"

"Excuse me."

At the same time as she heard and recognized the brown velvet voice, Willow saw, over Jamie's shoulders, a pair of long legs encased in fine charcoal-gray fabric.

She felt a surge of grim satisfaction: the man had returned at just the right time to be assaulted by the full force of her annoyance.

Grabbing Jamie's hand, she lurched upright, bursting

to vent the words of censure that were rising up inside her—

She gulped. And reared back. The stranger was way, way taller than she'd realized.

And he was *undoubtedly* the most devastatingly attractive man she had ever seen.

Her senses reeled from the dazzling effect of electric-blue eyes twinkling at her from under a slash of black eyebrows; Hollywood white teeth glinting in a wry smile; and features so perfectly chiseled they could have been computer-generated.

By Bill Gates himself.

But even as she gawked at him she had a disturbing feeling of déjà vu.

She had seen this man before.

Somewhere.

But if she had, wouldn't she have remembered him? He was surely unforgettable—

''Excuse me,'' he murmured again, a toe-curling, coaxing tone now brushing his velvety, sexy voice.

Willow stiffened her toes. And her knees. And her resolve. She was *not* going to allow this man to sweet-talk her. She was made, was she not, of sterner stuff?

She lasered him with an icy glare. ''Are those—'' she flicked her head curtly toward the trio who were still going at it hammer and tongs ''—your children?''

''Yeah.'' He raked a long-fingered hand through his black hair. Gold gleamed from his wafer-thin gold watch and from a stylishly engraved gold cuff link and from his wide gold wedding band. He dropped his hand and his hair fell back into perfect place—the unmistakable sign of a very expensive salon cut, Willow thought sourly. ''I have to confess,'' he murmured, ''they are most certainly mine—''

"Then I have to confess they are the very worst-behaved children I have ever seen!"

"If you'll let me apologize for them—"

"Apologize for *them?*" Her laugh was scornful. "Oh, don't apologize for *them.*" From the corner of her eye, she saw an employee approach to clean up the mess on the floor. "*You* are the one who should be ashamed. When children behave as yours do there's no one to blame but the parents!"

She should have stopped there. And she probably would, if she hadn't suddenly realized how pathetic she must seem to him in her cheap T-shirt and old cutoffs, while he looked elegant enough to have dinner at Buckingham Palace. So instead of calling a halt, she charged recklessly on.

"Maybe if you spent less time on your hair and your clothes and your...your fancy accessories," she sputtered, "and more time reading up on child psychology, you'd be able to take your family out into the world without *having* to apologize for them."

How rude! As soon as she'd said the words, she felt a shock of disbelief, and wanted desperately to drag them back. But of course it was too late...

And now he was angry.

A dangerous glitter had replaced the twinkle in his eyes. A thin, compressed line had replaced the full sensual curve of his mouth. And his pleasant demeanor had been replaced by an aura of hostile menace that made her think apprehensively of a cougar making ready to strike.

Uh-oh. Alarm rattled through her. A speedy retreat was most definitely called for.

Grabbing up Jamie's backpack, she stuck her nose in the air and in a valiant attempt to appear regal—which was a bit of a stretch considering her petite build and her ragtag outfit—she swept Jamie toward the exit door.

An imperious "Hey, hang on there!" rang after her.

She pretended not to hear it.

Once outside, she walked even faster in case he came after her, and hurried Jamie along the street, not looking back till they reached the end of the block. And when she did and saw no sign of him, she breathed a sigh of relief.

Thank goodness!

The whole incident, she reflected with a grimace, had been distressing to say the least.

Jamie said, "Who were they, Mom?"

"Just strangers. Passing through."

"Well, I'm glad about that because I sure wouldn't ever want to see them again."

Willow echoed his sentiments exactly.

Jamie dug into his pocket. "Here's your change."

"Put it in your bank," Willow said. "After your next swimming lesson, we'll go back to Morganti's again."

"Will we tell Gran what happened today?"

"Sure, if you like."

But when they got home, Willow's mother, Gemma, had news to pass on—news so welcome that both Willow and Jamie forgot all about the unfortunate incident at Morganti's.

The employment agency had called. At last Mrs. Trent had a job for Willow—an *excellent* job, she had enthused to Gemma, as nanny to a family of darling, *darling* children. Willow must call in at the office right away, her mother told her happily, to sign the new contract.

*   *   *

"The job's at *Summerhill?*" Appalled, Willow stared at Ida Trent.

"Yes, Willow. Do you have a problem with that?"

Willow's stomach dropped sickeningly as memories flooded her mind. Memories that still, after seven years, tore at her heart and filled it to overflowing with sorrow…and guilt.

More than anything, guilt. Guilt that would never, she knew, go away.

"Willow?"

With an effort, Willow gathered herself together. "Of course not. You know how keen I am to be working again."

Ida set her palms on the desk in front of her. "Good, because this job is perfect for you. And Summerhill is a *beautiful* house. Of course, it's been lying empty for the past seven years…the Galbraiths—Galen and Anna—moved to Nova Scotia right after their son's funeral, and then Galen suffered a fatal heart attack just days later. His wife never came back, and when she remarried this spring, the house passed on to the surviving son…Dr. Scott Galbraith. He arrived at Summerhill with his family a week ago."

"They're staying here permanently?"

"Yes. He's going into partnership with Dr. Black at the local clinic, starting first of next month. I know, Willow, that you prefer to be home at night, but he wants a live-in nanny and he's offering an *extremely* generous salary."

"And…you say you met the children?"

"Darling, *darling* children—" The phone rang and murmuring "Excuse me," Mrs. Trent picked it up. She listened to the caller and with a worried sigh, said, "Yes, Dora, of course. I'll be right there."

Putting down the phone, she pushed the contract across the desk to Willow.

"I'm sorry to rush you, dear." She got to her feet. "But I have to close the office and dash home. My husband has had one of his turns, that was his sitter."

Feeling disorientated, as if everything was happening a bit too fast, and she hadn't taken everything in yet, Willow scanned the contract and then signed her name.

As soon as she put down the pen, the agency owner said, "I really must hurry!"

Clasping her handbag, she ushered Willow to the door.

"Mrs. Trent, the children—"

"Darling, *darling* children," Mrs. Trent assured her again, with an unaccustomed vagueness. "Dr. Galbraith is expecting you at ten o'clock tomorrow morning. He'll fill you in on everything once you get to Summerhill."

The agency owner's white car was parked nearby. As she ran toward it, she added, over her shoulder, "The man's a widower, Willow, and he warned me not to send anyone who would see him as a potential husband. A plain-Jane nanny is what he asked for," she continued breathlessly, "and he more than hinted that women consider him devilishly attractive and find it difficult to keep their hands off him."

Willow gaped. The conceit of the man. Who did he think he was?

And as to that, it didn't do her own self-image much good to know Mrs. Trent considered her a plain-Jane. She knew she was no beauty but—

"I told him," the agency owner continued as she threw herself into her car, "that you had no interest in men." She slammed the car door. "So all in all," she called through the open window, "I think the relation-

ship will work out very well. You and Dr. Galbraith
would seem to be a perfect match!''

Mind still awhirl, Willow stood staring after the car
as it sped away. She was *not* looking for a husband;
Mrs. Trent had at least got *that* right. But…she and this
Scott Galbraith a perfect match? Hardly! Of all the men
in all the world she didn't want to work for, one as
arrogant as he apparently was would be at the top of
her list.

And of all the places in all of the world where she
didn't want to work, Summerhill would be right up
there, too.

She had no option, however, but to take the job, and
to work for him, because she desperately needed the
money.

Not only had bills piled up during her most recent
period of unemployment, but she'd had to take her car
off the road because she couldn't afford to renew the
insurance, and Gemma would need a car to drive Jamie
to school once the stormy winter weather set in. Being
the sole breadwinner for their household was a challenging and never-ending task; however, it was one she
was not about to shirk.

So she'd take this job and she'd turn up for work at
Summerhill tomorrow because she had no other choice.

But if Scott Galbraith were ever to discover that she
was responsible for the tragedy that had beset his family
seven years ago, he would boot her out of his house so
fast she wouldn't have time to blink!

The morning after the Morganti's fiasco, Scott woke
from a deep sleep to the sound of Mikey's demanding cry.

He rolled his eyes. Who needed an alarm clock with this kid in the house?

Lurching out of bed, he was stumbling to the door when Lizzie stormed into the room. She was holding a paperback in one hand and dragging her sister with the other.

"This little pest tore the last page out of my book!" She gave Amy a rough shake. "Before I'd even read it! Now she won't tell me where she put it!"

Scott said, "Lizzie, isn't that the book you bought at the library sale? The page might've been missing when—"

"I *didn't* tear her old book!" Amy managed to wrench herself free. "I like books. I'd never tear—"

Another demanding scream from Mikey's room drowned out whatever Amy had been going to say.

Scott tugged up the waistband of his cotton boxer shorts and made for the door. "Hang on, kids, we'll settle this after I change Mikey's diaper."

"Pest!" Lizzie hissed at her sister.

"Am not!"

"Are, too!"

Shaking his head, Scott went into Mikey's bedroom. His son and heir was jumping up and down in his crib, his pyjama bottoms at half-mast, weighed down by a soggy diaper. He stopped crying when he saw his father, and greeted him with a watery, heart-melting smile.

"Morning, buster," Scott said.

"Potty, Dad!"

Scott grinned. "I think we've missed the boat there, son!" He noticed that Mikey's blankets were scattered with scraps of paper. What the heck...?

Gathering up a few of the pieces, he scrutinized them and frowned as realization dawned.

"Mikey," he said. "Where did you get this?"

"Book."

"Lizzie's book? This is a page from Lizzie's book?"

"It fell out." He nodded gravely. "Amy said."

Out in the corridor, Scott heard Lizzie and her sister yelling at each other. Like a pair of heathens.

As he swept Mikey up and headed for the children's bathroom, he felt a great surge of thankfulness that this was going to be the last morning he'd have to cope alone with his rebellious troops. The new nanny—Mrs. Trent's promised "paragon of virtue"—was due to arrive at ten.

He could hardly wait.

Willow pedaled up the driveway to Summerhill on her bike, slowing as she reached the fork at the top. One road led to the forecourt of the Cape Cod house with its white siding and blue shuttered windows; the other led to the back.

The last—and only other time—she had ever visited this house, she had come not as an employee but as a highly distraught teenager with a letter to deliver.

The memory of that night, and the consequences of her actions, were still vivid in her mind. Far too vivid. And far too painful.

She shoved them back into their compartment and locked them up where they belonged. In the past.

She took the road to the rear of the house, where she parked her bike against the wall and then rang the doorbell. Taking in a deep breath to calm her nerves, she waited for someone to answer her summons.

She didn't have long to wait.

The door swung in and as it did, her tentative smile froze in place when she saw the person facing her. Her new employer was the man she'd confronted so rudely yesterday!

And with a suddenness that stole her breath away, she realized why she'd had that feeling of déjà vu at the sight of him. Yes, she *had* met Scott Galbraith before...and on this very spot.

The memory sent a chill shivering through her.

But no way would he recognize her. That long-ago night had been dark and moonless, and as she'd handed over the envelope, she'd skulked embarrassedly in the shadows.

No, he certainly wouldn't recognize her from seven years ago but he certainly recognized her from yesterday—and he seemed as stunned to see her as she was to see him.

"You!" His black eyebrows beetled in a scowl. "Don't tell me you're going to be my—"

"New nanny." Willow was grateful that the words came out in her normal voice rather than in the mousy squeak she'd half expected. "Yes. I'm Willow Tyler—"

From the interior of the house came a wail, followed by a shrill "Pest! Pest! Pest!" followed by an ominous crash.

"Welcome, Ms. Tyler, to Summerhill." Scott Galbraith's mouth twisted in a sardonic smile. "Yesterday, as I recall, you pronounced my children the worst-behaved you had ever seen." With an exaggeratedly courtly gesture, he invited her to come inside. "From now on, they are in your hands."

As she walked past him, her heart hammering like mad, he added, "I should warn you that in the past twenty months since their mother's death, my children have gone through no fewer than five top-notch nannies."

He closed the door firmly behind her.

Trapping her.

"I wonder," he continued in that already so-familiar brown velvet voice, "just how long *you* are going to last!"

CHAPTER TWO

TWELVE hours. That was how long she had lasted...

And, Willow reflected unhappily, she'd have to admit as much to Dr. Galbraith in the morning.

Fighting tears of misery and frustration, she stepped into the bath she'd run for herself in her en suite bathroom. *Nothing* was worth this hassle. The Galbraith children were monsters. They had absolutely defeated her attempts to get through to them and all day long had deliberately set themselves to provoke her.

But she'd been determined not to let them get the better of her and she'd really believed she had come out on top...until after she'd finally managed to settle them down for the night and had retired to her own room.

There, to her dismay, she had discovered that furtive little hands had been at work in her backpack. Oh, she could have forgiven the splodges of blue toothpaste gel squeezed over her best cream sweatshirt. She could even have forgiven the scarlet felt pen scrawls over every page of her new journal—a present from her mother. She could even have forgiven the broken chain of a favorite necklace. What she found *impossible* to forgive was the destruction of the last precious photograph of her father and herself, taken just weeks before he died.

Someone—Lizzie?—had tugged the picture from its brass frame and crumpled it into a crackly ball.

It was the final straw in a day straight out of hell.

And she needed to talk to someone about it!

There was a phone on her nightstand, and after her bath she put on her T-shirt nightie, and slumping down on the edge of the bed, called her mother and spilled out the whole dismal story.

Gemma Tyler "tsked" in all the right places, and when her daughter was finished, said softly, "Willow, the first day on a new job is very often the worst."

"I know, Mom. But I've had first days on new jobs before and not one was a tenth as bad as today. These kids are monsters, they really are."

"Tell me about them."

Willow wriggled onto the middle of the bed and lying back on her pillows, stared up at the ceiling. "The eldest, Lizzie, is blond and a true beauty. Her sister, Amy, has the loveliest curly red hair and big blue eyes. And Mikey looks so cute he could model diapers on TV—"

"They *sound* nice—"

"Looks are only skin deep, Mom. Lizzie's as hostile as she is beautiful, her sister shouts 'Black!' if I as much as think 'White'…and Mikey…that child bellows *'Not!'* at me every time he opens his little mouth!"

"Ah." Sympathy flowed across the line like a warm milk and honey drink. "I can see you have your work cut out for you. Tell me," Gemma continued before Willow had time to tell her she was quitting in the morning, "just one thing. When you look at these three children—I mean, *really* look at them—do you see at least a kernel of good in them?"

Willow crinkled her nose. A kernel of good? She wanted to say "No, absolutely not!" but she tried to be fair. And reluctantly she recalled that when she'd gone upstairs to check on the children during what she'd told them was to be their daily after-lunch "quiet time," instead of finding Mikey in his crib where she'd settled him she'd found him in Lizzie's room. Amy was there, too. The three were cuddled up asleep on top of Lizzie's bed...and Lizzie had her arms protectively around her two younger siblings.

The sight had touched something deep in Willow's soul.

But that had all gone by the wayside ten minutes later when the trio charged downstairs, squabbling and shoving and making so much racket they could have been an army.

"Ye...es, Mom. I do think there might be a *kernel* of good in them."

"Then you mustn't give up. These poor tots have lost their mother and it's only natural they'd fight against anyone who tried to take her place. You must give them a chance to work through their grief. And you must find a new place, for yourself, in their wounded hearts."

Wounded hearts.

Out of the blue, the words brought a tightness to Willow's throat and tears to her eyes as she remembered how wounded her own heart had been after her father had died.

And she knew, then, that she wouldn't run away from this daunting task that fate had sent her. She would stay on, at Summerhill, for as long as these children needed her.

"Good morning, Ms. Tyler."

"Good morning, Dr. Galbraith."

Scott leaned back against the counter, one hand wrapped around his coffee mug, as he regarded his new employee who had just raced into the kitchen. She'd come to a breathless halt and was darting a panicky glance around the room, taking in the harvest table with its empty chairs.

Flustered and flushed, she blurted out, "I'm sorry, I slept in and the children aren't in their rooms and—"

"Not a very good start." He sent her a look of challenge. "I hope this isn't going to be a regular occurrence?"

"No, of course not!" Her flush deepened. "I don't know what came over me."

"Perhaps my children are too much for you. They tired you out yesterday?"

She ran her hands nervously down the sides of her shorts. "The first day with a new family isn't always easy. But your children are definitely not too much for me. Now if you'll just tell me where they are—"

"Relax." He put down his mug and filled another one with coffee. "They've been fed and watered and they're in the den, watching TV. Lizzie's in charge. But you and I need to talk. Please sit down."

He saw wariness flicker in her eyes—wariness and anxiety.

What a funny little creature she was, he reflected as he set her mug on the table. If he'd had to choose one word to describe her, it would be "forgettable." Swiftly he ran a gaze over her and took in sandy sun-streaked hair scraped back in a neat ponytail. Eyes that couldn't make up their mind if they were green or gray. Nice skin but without a scrap of makeup other than a touch of pink lip gloss. And under her white T-shirt and perky pink shorts, the slim figure of a teenage boy.

As she slipped onto her seat and reached awkwardly for her coffee mug, he frowned. She hardly seemed the same person he'd had the altercation with in Morganti's.

Then she'd been all fire and spit and though she'd irritated the hell out of him, he'd had to admire her spunk. Now she looked ready to jump out of her skin.

He dragged out the chair opposite hers and sat down. "Ms. Tyler." He tried to keep the impatience from his voice. "Do you think I'm an ogre?"

She blinked. "No, of course not—"

"Ms. Tyler." He *rat-tatted* the fingers of one hand on the pine table surface. "If we're to have any kind of a working relationship, you're going to have to be honest with me. I'll ask you again, do you think I'm an ogre?"

She met his gaze steadily. "No, Dr. Galbraith, I don't."

"Well, good." He leaned back in his chair. "So—" he quirked one black eyebrow "—what *do* you think of me?"

"It's early days, Dr. Galbraith. I don't—"

"You must have formed some opinion!"

Ah, *now* he saw her eyes spark with the same fire he'd noticed at their first meeting.

"All right," she said. "Since you *insist* on knowing, I'll give you my opinion. I believe that ever since your wife's death you've been wallowing around in an absolute emotional mess and you're pretty sure your children are, too, especially Lizzie, so you've been cutting them all a lot of slack—way too much slack—and they've taken advantage of it. Are still taking advantage of it. And of you. In a nutshell, they're totally out of control—which is something a man like you finds intolerable but under the circumstances you're suffering it and this is putting even more stress on you. Oh, you're in quite a pickle, Dr. Galbraith. *Quite* a pickle."

Her words scraped still-tender scars off painful

wounds, exposing raw nerves that screamed in protest. He felt blood pound against his eardrums, but even as he struggled to curb his emotions, a surge of anger sent reason flying out the window.

The girl was outspoken and *way* out of line.

He would fire her.

His decision was swiftly made...the way he made most decisions. He was not, nor had he ever been, a ditherer.

But before he could tell her she was "out," he heard the thunder of approaching feet accompanied by Amy's screams and Lizzie's gratingly familiar "Pest! Pest! Pest!"

And as the noise reverberated in his head, he acknowledged—reluctantly, frustratedly, wearily—that firing Ms. Tyler was not an option. She was right. He *was* in a pickle, one *helluva* pickle. And though she was far too blunt for her own good, he had to admit he'd asked for it.

Furthermore, the reason she'd managed to upset him was that she'd hit the nail on the head...and the truth hurt.

Willow Tyler was as perspicacious as she was plain.

And she had survived a day that would have sent any of his previous five nannies running for the hills.

So after all, though Ms. Tyler had certainly got off to a bad start this morning, there was still a hope— however small that hope might be—that she would turn out to be the one person who could make his small family functional again.

"You certainly don't pull your punches," he said. "But I did ask for your opinion so I can't complain. I hope you'll always be as forthright with me. If there's one quality I appreciate in a person, it's honesty…and the flip side, of course, is that I can't tolerate deceit!''

He saw an odd expression flicker over her eyes—he thought for a moment it was fear, but he quickly dismissed the idea. She had told him the truth, so what did she have to be afraid of? Puzzled, he tried to figure out what it could have been…but before he could come up with an answer, he heard his storming troops thunder ever closer. With a wince, he forgot all about Ms. Tyler's odd expression and shoved himself up from the table.

''If you'll excuse me,'' he said hurriedly, ''I have to go out. I'll be back in the early afternoon.''

Feeling like a commander deserting on the eve of battle, he swiveled around and strode to the back door. Wrenching it open, he stepped outside and slammed the door shut just as his children erupted into the kitchen.

He stood on the stoop, leaning back against the door and sending up a prayer of gratitude for his timely escape.

Then inhaling a deep breath of the morning-scented air, he was about to leave when through the open window he heard the nanny say, in a clear and decidedly no-nonsense voice, ''Before we make any plans for the day, I want you to know how upset I was last night when I discovered that one or more of you had snuck into my room and destroyed some of my treasures.''

He froze where he stood. They'd sneaked into her room? They'd not only gone through her private things, but they had destroyed some of them?

Anger swelled up inside him. This was *intolerable*. He'd march inside right now and sort the little devils out. But good!

Wheeling around, he reached for the door handle. No way should she have to put up with—

He stopped himself just as he touched the knob.

And told himself to calm down.

Think it through.

And when he did, he realized it would be a major mistake to insert himself into the situation. He couldn't run interference every time the children misbehaved. It would ruin any hope Ms. Tyler had of gaining their respect.

In the long run, it would do more harm than good.

So he stood there a little while longer, listening, then he turned away from the door and made his way to the three-car detached garage that sat on the grounds at the westerly side of the house.

"So...is that understood?" Willow stood over the children, who were clustered in a hostile group by the kitchen table. "We all have our own areas of privacy, and those areas are sacrosanct."

"What's sacrosanct?" muttered Amy.

"It's what she said." Lizzie sounded sullen. "We don't go there. It's private. We don't touch stuff that belongs to other people. Just like you should never have touched my book and ripped out the page!"

"I didn't!" Amy cried. "I told you last night, it just fell out and I put it in Mikey's crib so you—"

"Children." Willow gritted her teeth. "Let's move on, shall we? Let's start over. It's a new day."

Lizzie avoided looking at her. "Where's Dad?"

"He went out."

Lizzie frowned. "Where did he go?"

"He didn't say," Willow responded lightly. "But since it's such a lovely day, we'll all go out, too."

"Don't *wanna* go out!" Amy fisted her hands on her hips. "Wanna watch TV!"

"Me, too!" Mikey dumped himself solidly down on his bottom, his attitude screaming *I'm on strike!*

"We'll go for a swim." Willow opened the fridge and took out a jar of peanut butter. Scooping a bag of buns from the bread bin, she said, "We'll pack a lunch and have a picnic after."

Lizzie finally raised her eyes and fixed her with a scornful gaze. "We *can't* go for a swim. Dad says it's too late in the season to bother opening up the Summerhill pool!"

Willow slit the buns and began spreading them with peanut butter. "We're not going to be using your pool." She rummaged in the cupboard, found a jar of honey and screwed off the lid. "Now would you run upstairs, Lizzie, and fetch all the swimsuits?"

"How do you know we've got any!" Amy screwed up her freckled little nose. "We might not!"

"Not!" bawled Mikey.

"If you don't have any swimsuits," Willow said in an airy tone, "then you'll all have to skinny-dip!"

Lizzie gaped. "You can't make us!"

Willow slathered honey atop the peanut butter. "You'll have the choice of skinny-dipping or going into the water with your clothes on. It's up to you." She focused her gaze on the buns as she sliced them into neat quarters.

"We've got swimsuits." Lizzie's tone was dour.

"Good!" Willow packed the sandwiches in a plastic bag.

"But," Lizzie sneered, "we won't be using them to-day because we're not *allowed* to go in public swimming pools! Our last nanny said that's where people pick up all sorts of things like athlete's foot and…other dangerous bugs!''

"So there!" Amy was triumphant. "We're not allowed."

"Not!" echoed Mikey.

"We won't be going to a public pool." Willow arranged the bag of sandwiches in her backpack.

"Then where *are* we going?" Lizzie's chin had a belligerent jut.

"It's a surprise." Willow regarded her charges with a pleasant smile. "But I think you're going to enjoy it."

Scott got home around two and as soon as he walked into the kitchen, he spotted the note propped against the fruit basket on the harvest table.

Dr. Galbraith,
   I've taken the children to the creek, to play in the shallower water down below the swimming hole.

How was his new nanny coping? he wondered. He could just imagine the protestations she'd been subjected to when she'd suggested a swim. No matter *what* she'd suggested, the arguments would have been the same. And if the kids hadn't objected in so many words, they'd have expressed their hostility in attitude. He'd seen them in action untold times, with the previous five nannies.

It might be interesting, he reflected, to take a stroll through the forest, and sneak a peek at the situation.

The swimming hole was on the Galbraith estate, and because of the craggy cliff that rose from the far bank, the area was inaccessible to the public and could be reached only via a private trail through the woods from Summerhill.

He hadn't been near the old swimming hole in years; and he wondered, idly, how Ms. Tyler even knew of its existence.

Willow packed away the picnic things and stood for a moment watching the children frolic in the shallow waves that washed over the smooth sun-warmed sandy beach.

It had been difficult for her to come here. She'd found it distressing to walk past the deep secluded pool where she and Chad had spent so many secret hours swimming together as teenagers—but she'd known her charges would love playing in the water and on the sandy beach so she'd made the effort. And now she was glad. They'd had fun.

They made a colorful picture, she mused as she watched them splash around in their expensive designer togs, Lizzie in her yellow bikini, Amy in a blue one-piece, Mikey in his neon-orange shorts.

She should have brought her camera. She would, when they came back another day.

But it was time now to be heading home, so she should be calling to them to come and get dried off and dressed.

First, though, she should put her own clothes on.

She slipped behind a leafy bush high enough to give her some privacy from the children but not too high that she couldn't see over it to check on them.

She slipped off her bikini…and then, on an impulse, stretched up her arms to the sky, relishing the unfamiliar and primitive sensation of being naked in the golden sun—

A twig crackled nearby.

Her pulse gave an erratic jump, and when she slewed her gaze to where the sound had come from, she felt her heart stop. Scott Galbraith was standing as if frozen to the spot, just three yards away on the fringe of the forest, his blue eyes staring at her with as much shock as she knew must be glittering in her own.

Suppressing a horrified gasp, she swept up her towel and screened herself from the neck down. Her cheeks felt as if they were on fire; her heartbeats scrambled out of control. She clamped her jaw to keep from yelping "What are *you* doing here?" and waited tensely for him to make a move.

He grimaced.

And then muttering something under his breath, he took a step backward.

"I'm sorry." His voice was thick, his tone filled with abject apology. "I didn't mean...I only walked over to...I just thought I'd—oh, *dammit,* Ms. Tyler," he sputtered. "I hadn't a clue that you'd be...I hadn't a clue I'd find you..."

"Naked?" Willow's voice came out as coolly as she'd ordered it to—and with just the right touch of wry amusement. "Dr. Galbraith, this is surely not the first time you've seen a nude woman. And I'm sure it won't be the last. Now if you'll excuse me, I have to get dressed and attend to your children."

He looked as if he was going to say something more.

Again she waited. And *willed* him to leave.

In the end, he scratched a hand clumsily through his hair, twisted his face in an expression of excruciating embarrassment, before turning away with one last muttered "Sorry," and disappearing into the forest.

Willow's breath quivered out in a whimper of relief.

He was gone.

Thank heaven.

But…oh Lord…what a disaster!

How on *earth* was she going to face the man now? Now that he'd seen her with nothing on but her watch!

Scott crashed through the woods, wondering if he'd ever felt so stupid. What a blundering idiot. Served him right, for snooping. He'd got more than he bargained for. Far more.

How was he going to face her now?

And would he ever again be able to look at her without picturing her naked? He groaned. If only he'd turned up five minutes later. If only he hadn't walked out of the trees just as she'd stretched her arms up to the skies, gilded in sunshine like a wood nymph, without a stitch of clothing and her smooth skin tanned to a deliciously dusky brown except for the stark white areas where her bikini—

Oh damn, damn, damn!

He punched one hand into the palm of the other. Willow Tyler had told him that morning that he was in a pickle. He snorted. A pickle was *mild* compared to the situation he was in now.

He'd asked Ida Trent to send him a plain-Jane nanny. A plain-Jane nanny she was not. It wasn't that she was a looker; in fact, hadn't he already decided her face was eminently forgettable? The problem was…her figure. It was exquisite. The most exquisite he'd ever seen and— she was right about one thing!—he'd seen more than a few naked ladies in his day! But he just couldn't have this girl prancing around the house in skimpy T-shirts and shorts now that he knew what she looked like underneath.

He needed to suit her up in armor—some kind of armor that would obliterate the sexy image from his mind.

He pondered the problem as he emerged from the trees and started walking up the path to the house. And then, just as he reached the back door, the solution came to him.

The nannies who'd worked for him in the city had worn uniforms ordered from the smartnannies.com catalog—each outfit consisting of a crisp blue dress, with white collar and cuffs; white stockings; white lace-up shoes.

And that, of course, was the answer. He would put Ms. Tyler in a uniform. Then she'd blend in with the woodwork. And far from being stimulated to fantasize about her, he wouldn't even see her!

It would work.

He groaned again and rolled his eyes heavenward.

It *had* to work!

"Ms. Tyler, could you come into my study for a moment?"

Willow paused at the foot of the stairs, her stomach sinking. Dr. Galbraith had kept scrupulously out of her way for the rest of the day after the creek incident and she'd hoped she could escape to her room for the night without having encountered him. Her hopes were not to be realized.

Indicating the pile of clothing and towels clutched in her arms, she said, "Okay if I put these in the washer first?"

"Sure, go ahead." He withdrew into his study again, but left the door open.

Willow hurried along to the laundry room, wondering

what he was going to say. Was he going to fire her?
Did he think her behavior that afternoon had
been…unbecoming? Well, she'd find out soon enough!

After setting the washer going, she brushed a nervous
hand over her hair, making sure her ponytail was tidy,
before making her way reluctantly through to the study.

She gave a light *rat-tat* on the door and walked in.

Her employer was pacing restlessly, his head down,
his hands jammed into his trouser pockets.

As she entered, he halted and jerked his head up.

"Ah, there you are." He looked as ill at ease as she
felt. And that gave her confidence a slight boost. She
said, quietly,

"You wanted to see me."

"I wanted to tell you that the cook/housekeeper I've
hired—a Mrs. Caird—will be starting tomorrow. She'll
do all the cooking plus all the housework, except for
your laundry and the children's, and the cleaning of
your room. Will that be satisfactory?"

Willow nodded, feeling dizzy with relief that she still
had her job. "Of course. But…I'll have the run of the
kitchen, for making snacks for the children and so on?"

"That's something you can arrange with Mrs. Caird.
I'm sure she'll have no objections as long as you clean
up after yourself."

"Thank you." Willow turned away and started toward the door.

"Er…before you disappear again…there's something
I…need to know."

Willow turned around, questioningly. But when she
saw the evasive expression in his eyes, she felt a quiver
of apprehension. Was he going to chastise her, now, for
her immodest behavior that afternoon?

"Ye…es," she said. "And what is that?"

"I need to…know…er…your measurements."

"I don't understand. What measurements?"

A vein throbbed at his right temple. "Do I need to spell it out?" He scowled at her. And dark color seeped into his cheeks. "The usual measurements, for heaven's sake!"

"The…usual measurements?"

"The size, Ms. Tyler, of your waist, and your hips. And—" he looked as if he was going to choke on the words but finally he got them out "—the size of your breasts."

CHAPTER THREE

HELL will freeze over first!

Willow tried to sputter the words out but her voice wouldn't cooperate. Her *body* measurements? Wasn't it bad enough that the man had caught her naked...now he wanted to know her *bust* size? His boldness beggared belief! What kind of a sleazy—

"I—" He shifted his feet awkwardly. "I want to put you in an *outfit* and since I have to order it from a catalog—"

"An *outfit,* Dr. Galbraith?" At last she'd found her voice but it was so stunned she hardly recognized it. "What *kind* of an outfit? Do you see me perhaps in a crimson lace bra with a black and crimson garter belt and...and...sheer black stockings with red sparkly high-heeled shoes...and—"

"I meant...a *uniform,* Ms. Tyler." The man sounded as if he had a fishbone stuck in his craw. "A *nanny's* uniform, of the type my children's previous nannies wore. Ordered through the smartnannies.com catalog on the Internet."

Willow wanted to shrivel up and disappear. A nanny's uniform. What an absolute idiot she'd made of herself.

"I apologize." Her cheeks must be as crimson as the scanty lace bra her imagination had so vividly conjured up. "We seem to have been talking at cross-purposes."

"Yes," he murmured. "It would seem we have."

But, she reflected defensively, it hadn't been totally

her fault. He should have made himself clear, instead of bumbling along like an embarrassed teenager. With a touch of asperity, she said, "Did none of your previous nannies balk at providing you with such... personal...information?"

"I always left that kind of stuff to my stepmother. She did the hiring of the nannies...and the ordering of their uniforms. This is all new to me, Ms. Tyler. I'd appreciate if you'd make some allowances!"

His sudden smile was as unexpected as it was disarming: a curve of sensual lips, a flash of white teeth, a twinkle of wickedly blue eyes. The smile not only dazzled her, but it almost felled her. When Scott Galbraith set out to charm—as he was obviously doing now!—he was irresistible.

And when she stared, transfixed, into those arresting blue eyes, she realized with a bone-chilling sense of alarm that if she let her guard down, how dangerously easy it would be to let herself fall in love with him. She sensed herself teetering on the edge of it already—as if she were balancing in the open doorway of a plane at thirty thousand feet, with no parachute strapped to her back.

And falling for Dr. Scott Galbraith would be the worst mistake she had ever made.

No, the second worst. The worst mistake was the one she'd made seven years ago, when she had—with such tragic consequences—mistaken teenage infatuation for true love.

He was speaking again, and drawing in a shivery breath, she dragged her thoughts from the past and forced herself to concentrate.

"Tell you what," he said. "Since you seem so averse to giving me your measurements, I'll set you up at my

computer and you can input your order yourself." He
started toward his desk. "Would you find that acceptable?"

"No."

He halted and regarded her with a surprised expression.

"You don't want to input the info yourself?" he
asked.

"I'd…prefer not to wear a uniform."

"Why not?"

"It would come between me and the children."

"Ms. Tyler, they're accustomed to their nannies being in uniform. If anything, it would give them a feeling
of continuity, which could only be good."

"Granted, but it would also set me apart, which could
only be bad."

"It would give you an aura of authority," he argued,
"which would help you to establish control."

"From what you've told me," she said, "wearing a
uniform didn't help the previous nannies in that regard!
Besides," she added, "a uniform might be appropriate
in a city setting but here…"

"Yes?"

"I can't see myself in a uniform while I splash
around in the creek with the children, or while we play
hide-and-seek in the woods. Can you?"

He stared at her with a perplexed expression, as if
she'd posed a highly complex problem.

"I'll order a couple of uniforms," he said finally.
"And you'll give it your best shot. If after one week,
you find it too…cumbersome…for certain activities,
then we'll discuss the matter again and come up with a
compromise that satisfies us both. Is that acceptable?"

"Yes," she said, but without any great enthusiasm. "That would be acceptable."

"Okay, let's get this show on the road." He took his seat at the desk, in front of the computer.

She should have been watching the screen as he accessed the Web site, instead she found herself looking down at the top of his head…and noticing how rich his black hair was, and how much silkier it seemed, up close—

He rose from his chair. "Sit down."

She did, and felt his warmth lingering on the padded leather seat. There was an intimacy about it that she found disconcerting. Wriggling impatiently, she shifted her mind to a higher plane as he crossed to the window and stood with his back to her.

After she'd input her info, she rolled back the swivel chair and got to her feet.

She said, to the back of his head and his impressively wide shoulders, "It seems a bit stupid now…"

He turned. "What does?"

"That I made such a fuss about giving out my measurements." She gave an ironic chuckle and added, almost to herself, "It's not as if I've that much to hide!"

As soon as she'd spoken, she wished the words unsaid. Thanks to her strip-show at the creek, her employer knew exactly how much—or, rather, how *little!*—she had to hide. And she knew, by the shadow darkening his blue eyes, that reminding him of it had not been one of her better ideas.

He thrust his hands into his trouser pockets, and she heard the impatient jingle of coins or keys. The sound was as dismissive as the ring of a school bell.

"Will that be all?" she asked.

"Just one more thing. This morning I drove to

Crestville to visit my in-laws and I've invited them here for dinner. On Friday. That'll give Mrs. Caird time to get used to my kitchen before she has to cook for guests, and it will give you the best part of a week to lick my children into some kind of shape so they don't disgrace me too deplorably. Do you think you can do that?''

Willow hadn't been aware that his in-laws lived in Crestville, a town about fifty miles up the highway. "I'll certainly do my best."

"That's all I can *ask*. But," he added, and flashed her another of his debilitating smiles, "I can *hope* for a miracle!"

A series of warm tingles fluttered Willow's senses as she was exposed to the full force of his charm. Did Scott Galbraith have *any* idea what a heartbreaker he was?

But even as she asked herself the question, she recalled what Ida Trent had said about the man believing himself to be "devilishly attractive" to the opposite sex. The memory frosted the warm glow that had suffused her skin. And instead of fainting at his feet as she'd momentarily felt prone to do, she returned crisply,

"Hope, as they say, springs eternal! Now, will that be all?"

"Yes, that will be all. Good night, Ms. Tyler."

"Good night, Dr. Galbraith."

As she drew the door closed behind her, she heard him add, very softly, "Try to get to bed early, Ms. Tyler. We wouldn't want your sleeping in to become a habit."

Next morning, Willow's alarm went off at seven.

Yawning, she flicked it off and got up. Then she wandered sleepily across the plush pink carpet to the window and drew back the luxuriously heavy pink drapes.

It was dreary outside. A wild gale was blowing and rain lashed the countryside in gunmetal-gray sheets. Unless the storm eased up later, it would be too wet to take the children out. She'd be cooped up in the house with the little monsters. The prospect made her shudder.

But as she padded toward the en suite bathroom—past the bed with its pink-sprigged duvet and past the elegant white wicker furniture—she experienced a sudden rush of pleasure. How *lucky* she was to have such beautiful quarters. Quite a change from home, where space was at a premium—and walking barefoot over toy-littered floors was as risk-fraught as crossing a minefield!

After showering, she dressed in jeans and an aqua sweatshirt and then set out to check on her charges.

She was almost at Mikey's room, which was next door to her own, when she heard a fretful cry.

She pushed the door open and switched on the light.

The sudden brightness took the child aback, and his cry stopped in midstream. As Willow entered the room, she saw him standing up in his crib, his cheeks scarlet, his eyes pearled with tears, his hands clutching the crib rail.

He stared at her for ten long seconds, then he released the crib rail and plumped down onto his bottom. Lower lip jutting, he watched warily as she approached the crib.

Willow set her hands on the top rail and looked down at him with a smile. "Hi," she said. "Good morning!"

He scowled. *"Not!"*

She laughed. "You're right. Actually it's not. It's

raining and it looks as if it might be on for the duration!
Now,'' she said, ''let's get your diaper changed and—''

"Dry!"

She lowered the side of the crib and leaning over,
checked his diaper and found it was, indeed, dry.
"What a good boy!" She looked at him admiringly.
"Aren't you clever!"

His face creased in a delighted smile. "I clever!"

He was so like his father! He had the same electric-
blue eyes, the same heart-stealing smile. What a cute
little guy he was. And of *course* he wasn't a monster.
How could she ever have thought he was!

"Up!" he demanded. "Potty!"

"Right!" She swung him up and gave him a big hug.
He grabbed her hair, and snuggled his face in it, sniffing
it.

"So we're friends now?" she asked as she carried
him out to the passage and across to the large bathroom
shared by the three children.

She felt his arms go around her neck. Felt his lips
against her skin as he pressed his open mouth to her
cheek.

His response was muffled so she couldn't make out
what he was saying. But she didn't need to.

His message was clear.

Scott zipped up his jeans, and fastening the metal button
at the waistband, headed for his bedroom door.

Stepping out into the passage, he caught sight of his
new nanny. She was crossing to the children's bathroom
from Mikey's room and she had his son in her arms.
Even from twenty feet away, he could sense the rapport
between them.

It didn't surprise him. Mikey was usually pretty easy

to win over when his sisters weren't around. Ms. Tyler would find the girls a much bigger challenge. But at least, he mused as she disappeared from sight, she had made a start.

Checking on his daughters, he found them still asleep. Whistling under his breath, he made his way to the kitchen. After putting on coffee, he boiled an egg for Mikey, made toast and fried a batch of eggs and tomatoes and hash browns while he nuked rashers of bacon in the microwave.

By the time he heard Ms. Tyler come down the stairs, everything was ready and the table set.

"Good timing," he said as she came in. "I'm just finished."

The nanny's straight little nose crinkled. "I thought, when I smelled the bacon, that Mrs. Caird had arrived early!"

Her eyes looked more green than gray today, he noted absently—probably reflecting the color from her aqua sweatshirt. Quite pretty eyes, with incredibly long feathery lashes, a shade or two darker than her sandy hair.

"Dad!" Mikey strained toward him.

He stepped over and scooped the child from her arms—and got a whiff of whatever perfume she was wearing. It was soft and powdery. Feminine. It made him want to nuzzle his face into her neck, the way he'd seen Mikey do earlier!

And how totally inappropriate that would be. Grounds for a sexual harassment suit...

He squelched the wayward urge.

"Hi, Mikey." He dropped a kiss on his son's head before strapping the child into his high chair. "And good morning to you, Ms. Tyler. No, Mrs. Caird won't be here till after lunch. Pour yourself a coffee, and I'll feed Mikey."

He peeled the toddler's egg, dropped it into a bowl and chopped it up, before setting the bowl on Mikey's white plastic tray along with a few fingers of buttered toast.

In the meantime, Ms. Tyler had poured her coffee and was hovering.

"I must admit," she said, "that I'm surprised to find you so...at home...in the kitchen."

"Did you think I was just a hewer of wood and a drawer of water?" He grinned. "Heck no, I'm a New Age Man. Able to turn my hand to any household task you care to mention."

Waving her toward a chair, he said, "I hope you're hungry."

As she perched on the chair, he opened the oven door and withdrew two plates arranged with the bacon, over-easy eggs, hash browns and tomato wedges he'd prepared earlier. Setting a plate in front of her, he murmured, *"Bon appétit."*

And setting the other plate down on the table across from her, he took his own seat.

She looked at her plate with a dazed expression.

"Dig in," he said.

"I...usually just have coffee in the morning. But...I must admit, this is very tempting..."

"Coffee's not a food, Ms. Tyler. As long as you're under my roof, you'll eat properly. And that means, no skipping breakfast. Understood?"

Her tone had a mischievous edge as she said, "Then perhaps we should have held off on ordering my uniform...or perhaps we should reorder now. The next size up!"

He deliberately sidestepped any further discussion of uniforms. "Believe me," he said, "no matter how heartily you may eat, my brood will keep you so busy running after them you won't put on a single ounce. I guarantee it."

"Then—" she lowered her eyes demurely to her plate as she picked up her fork "—we'll stick with the Small."

Out of nowhere, he was suddenly visited by an image of her petite figure, stretching naked in the sunlight. The memory was vivid. Tantalizingly vivid.

He felt a stirring of desire and decided it was time—past time!—to change the subject completely.

"Tell me, Ms. Tyler, the little boy you were with at Morganti's the other day...was he one of your charges?"

She dropped a morsel of bacon from her fork, and it fell into her mug. Her cheeks turned pink and she made a vexed *tsking* sound. She seemed to take an inordinate length of time to rescue the bacon scrap from the coffee. Only after she'd achieved her goal and finally transferred the scrap to the edge of her plate did she look up at him.

Her eyes were blank of emotion as she gazed at him levelly. "He's my son."

"Your *son?*"

"I'd assumed Mrs. Trent would have filled you in on my background."

"Mrs. Trent filled me in on your credentials, and your experience, but...no, she didn't mention that you have a child. Who's looking after him at present? His father?"

The pink in her cheeks had faded away, leaving her

skin pale. Paler than it had been before. "His father…isn't involved. My mother looks after Jamie."

"Does the guy at least give you financial support?"

"No." Lowering her gaze to her plate, she toyed with her hash browns. When she looked up again, her gaze was still shuttered. "He's no longer in my life. I'm a single mom, yes, but that's not going to affect how I carry out my work here. I have everything under control."

He nodded. "Good."

And for the next few minutes they ate. He cleared his plate, and brushed his napkin over his mouth, before starting up the conversation again.

"Where," he asked, "does your mother live?"

"We rent a house at the east end of town. It's small, but the area's quiet. My mother's been a widow for some years—her health isn't all that good so she doesn't go out to work. She enjoys staying home and looking after Jamie."

"How old is the boy?"

"Six."

"In between Lizzie and Amy. But," he added with a self-deprecatory twist of his lips, "judging by what I saw of him at Morganti's, much better behaved." He raised his eyebrows. "Maybe you could bring him up here sometime? He might be a good influence."

"I…don't think that would be a good idea."

"Why not?"

"It might be unsettling for Jamie. Your children are privileged. I wouldn't want him to become dissatisfied with his own situation."

"You think that might happen?"

"It's not a chance I want to take. But thank you," she continued, with a stiff smile, "for your invitation."

"I'm sorry you won't accept. When Lizzie starts school here in September and Amy starts kindergarten, it might've made it easier for them if they'd already met one of the other children."

"Dr. Galbraith." She arranged her fork and knife neatly on her plate. "That sounds to me remarkably like emotional blackmail. Are you trying to send me on a guilt trip?"

He chuckled. "Yeah. That was exactly what I was trying to do. It's not going to work?"

"No. It's not going to work. Besides, I like to keep my private life separate from my professional life. It makes things less...complicated."

"And you don't like complicated?"

"Uh-uh. Simple. That's how I like things to be."

While they'd been talking, Mikey had been fully occupied eating his breakfast. Now he was finished and with a sweeping flourish, he threw his plastic mug across the room. By chance, it landed in the sink.

"Clever boy!" He clapped his hands.

As he did, the kitchen door burst open and Amy and Lizzie erupted into the room. Amy was crying, Lizzie was taunting.

Scott pushed up to his feet.

"Good morning, girls," he said over the din. "Breakfast's ready, sit down and Ms. Tyler will serve it."

As he passed her on his way to the door he murmured, "I'm going down to the clinic, see you later," and added, under his breath, "Good luck!"

Willow phoned Jamie from the wall phone in the kitchen after she'd served Amy and Lizzie their breakfast and after she'd set Mikey on the floor to play with his farmyard set.

While she talked to her son, Mikey chatted happily to his collection of cows and horses; but although Amy and Lizzie *appeared* just as engrossed in their bacon and eggs, she sensed they were listening to her every word.

Half turning away, Willow chatted for a minute or two with her mother, who then passed the phone to Jamie.

"Hi, honey." Willow smiled as she imagined her son with the phone in his hands, his eyes sparkling with excitement. "How's it going?"

"I miss you, Mom!"

"I miss you too, sweetie. Are you being good for Gran?"

"Well I stepped on her corn by accident yesterday but she said it was okay. And I bet I'm behaving better than the kids at Summerhill! Are they insuff'rable?"

Willow bit back a chuckle. Jamie's use of big words never failed to amuse her. "No," she said. "Not really."

"You'll whip them into shape, right?"

She laughed. "Something like that. So what are you going to do today?"

"Gran's taking me for my swimming lesson, then we're going to Morganti's. My treat. I told her. With your money. Is that okay?"

"Yes, that's fine, Jamie. Enjoy yourself, and I'll talk to you again tomorrow."

She noticed that while she'd been chatting, the *click-click* of spoon against china from the table had gradually ceased and she suspected that the girls had become so involved with her conversation, they'd stopped eating.

The moment she hung up, she heard the sound of renewed activity, and when she turned around, they both had their heads bent over their plates and were scooping their breakfasts into their mouths as fast as if they had a train to catch.

Amused, she crossed to the sink and started tidying up. Outside, the rain still lashed down, but she hoped, as she heard Amy and Lizzie renew their bickering, that the weather would clear up before too long.

It did.

The rain tapered away around eleven and after having spent most of the morning refereeing Amy and Lizzie's skirmishes, and coping with their open and sometimes nasty hostility to her, she took her charges out for a walk.

As she led them toward the woods that stretched to the west of the property, Mikey clung to her hand and resisted his sisters' attempts to win him back to their camp.

"Come with me," Lizzie coaxed. "Take *my* hand."

"Not!" he said. And clung even more tightly to Willow.

Lizzie snorted and looked at him scornfully. "Little suck!" she muttered under her breath and stalked ahead.

"Suckie brat!" Amy hissed. And ran after her sister.

But Lizzie didn't want anything to do with her and veered away when Amy would have walked alongside her.

Willow finally got the trio involved in a game of hide-and-seek, and after a slow start, they played boisterously until it was time to return to the house for lunch.

They walked home in a group, with Willow carrying Mikey piggyback after he announced that his legs were "falling down." At that, Amy laughed, and even Lizzie couldn't keep back a smile.

"It's not your legs that are falling down, stupid," she said. "It's you!"

"Lizzie," Willow said gently, "sometimes Mikey will say things that *you* may think are stupid...but please don't ever call him stupid again. He's a smart little boy...but even if he weren't, it's not a nice name to call anyone. Okay?"

"Okay," Lizzie mumbled. And actually added, "Sorry, Mikey. I know you're not stupid."

"I clever!" Mikey announced proudly. "Clever boy!"

"Yes." Lizzie patted his knee. "You are. A very clever boy!"

In comparative harmony, they walked the rest of the way home, and in comparative harmony, they ate lunch, after which Willow settled the children upstairs for their "quiet time."

When she ran downstairs again, she saw her employer coming out of his study. With him was a middle-aged woman with graying brown hair. Her spare figure was neatly attired in a wraparound dress the same gold color as her eyes—friendly eyes that fixed with interest on Willow.

"Ah, there you are, Ms. Tyler." Scott Galbraith ushered the woman forward. "Come and meet our new housekeeper. Mrs. Caird, this is Willow Tyler, the children's nanny."

Willow said "Hi," and accepted the other woman's offered hand. Mrs. Caird's long fingers were warm and bony.

"I've given Mrs. Caird the apartment above the garage," Dr. Galbraith said to Willow. "And I've already shown her over her quarters and carried up her luggage. I was just about to give her a tour of the house, but perhaps you'd like to do that, Ms. Tyler, it'll give the two of you a chance to get acquainted—"

He broke off as the phone rang in his study.

"Excuse me," he said. And went back into his study.

The new housekeeper's brows tugged together as she turned her attention to Willow. "I don't think we've met before, but your name's familiar to me. I believe a young lad I fostered may have been at high school with you. His name was Daniel. Daniel Firth."

Willow's heart gave a sickening lurch, but she managed to say lightly, "I didn't really know Daniel—he was two years ahead of me. Didn't he move away a while back?" she asked, trying to divert the woman's focus from herself.

"Yes, he's working in Toronto." The housekeeper's frown deepened. "I know he spoke of you at one time—but in what connection, I just can't think. It'll come back to me, though," she added. "It always does. Eventually!"

Willow forced a bright smile. "Shall we have that tour now?" she asked, her tone polite but making it clear she wasn't interested in any more chitchat.

"Yes, I should like to see my kitchen."

As Willow led the housekeeper along the passage, she felt the beginning of a pounding headache. She and Dan Firth hadn't been friends but Dan and Chad *had* been friends. Close friends. The only person closer to Chad had been herself. *Their* relationship, however, had been a tightly guarded secret...one Chad had shared only with Dan, and only because he'd needed Dan to cover for him on the occasions when he went out at night to meet Willow.

Had Dan let slip a hint of this secret to his foster mother? Goose bumps prickled Willow's skin. Whatever the woman knew, she seemed confident it would come back to her.

Meanwhile Willow was doomed to spend her days at Summerhill with a menacing time bomb ticking away unseen.

One that could cause havoc with her life, and change it forever, if it exploded.

CHAPTER FOUR

"AH, THERE you are, Ms. Tyler!"

It was the following afternoon. The children were having their "quiet time," and Willow had just finished pinning a hamper of clothes to the line in the backyard when she heard her boss address her.

She glanced around and saw him on the back door step, his tall, lean figure shown off to perfection in a sports shirt and taupe Bermuda shorts.

Her legs suddenly felt as limp as the washing she'd just pinned to the line...and when he started walking toward her, she was alarmed to find herself wondering what it would feel like to be enfolded tenderly in his arms.

Was she out of her *mind?* Dr. Scott Galbraith had specifically asked for a nanny who wouldn't swoon over him. A plain-Jane nanny who wasn't man mad. She had never *considered* herself man mad, but where *this* man was concerned, she really had to wonder!

"My sister-in-law's here," he said. "Camryn Moffat. We're going to play a round of golf but she's agreed to baby-sit for half an hour first so I can take you out for a trial run in my other car."

His businesslike tone knocked Willow abruptly back to her senses. "Which other car?" she asked, raising a hand to shield her eyes from the sun.

"It was my father's car. It's been sitting in the garage since my parents left Summerhill. I had it serviced last week. You can have it for driving the kids around, and

54

for going home on your time off. I want to take you for a spin now, to give you a chance to get used to the vehicle.''

"And I'm guessing," she returned in a deliberately arch tone, "that you also want to know if I'm a maniac behind the wheel!''

"Are you?"

"You'll soon find out!"

"I'll be sure to buckle my safety belt!" he said dryly. "Ready to go?"

It was a roasting hot day and Willow had dressed for comfort. But now, looking down at her skimpy tank top and her denim cutoffs, she murmured, "I should change first.''

"You're fine.''

She didn't feel fine; she felt awkward and drab…and plain. But plain was good, wasn't it? Plain was what Dr. Scott Galbraith wanted in a nanny, wasn't it? So she should be *delighted* that she was so right for the job!

Hiding a wry smile, she followed him inside, and then they walked together through to the front hall.

When they got there, Willow smelled the faintest drift of perfume lingering in the air—jasmine and roses. Tantalizing, rich. Camryn Moffat's scent. Had to be.

"You'll meet my sister-in-law when we get back." Scott Galbraith opened the front door. "She's gone upstairs to look in on the kids.''

When Willow stepped outside, the first thing she saw was a dashing blue convertible parked at a jaunty angle by the foot of the steps. Camryn Moffat's car. Had to be.

It was apparent that the woman enjoyed the same kind of luxurious lifestyle as her brother-in-law.

And if his businesslike demeanor hadn't already knocked Willow to her senses, seeing this ultraexpensive vehicle would have. She acknowledged that she'd be crazy to spend one single second drooling over her employer. Even if she had room for a man in her life—which she didn't—Scott Galbraith was way, way out of her league.

Just as his stepbrother Chad had been.

She'd known that at the time, but still she'd allowed herself to be tempted into an affair with him. The memory of how disastrously that affair had turned out sobered her now as nothing else could.

And so, after she was settled in the driver's seat in the car, it took little effort to focus all her attention on the dashboard and familiarize herself with it.

Once she had, she turned the key in the ignition.

"Right," the man beside her said as the engine purred to life. "Let's take a drive up the Crestville road, see how you handle her on the highway."

Willow backed the car out of the garage, keeping well away from his green luxury vehicle, which was parked right next to it.

She wasn't nervous about this "trial run." She knew she was a good driver...and her boss would soon know it, too.

It had been a huge mistake, taking her out in the car while she was wearing these damned cutoff shorts. When she'd asked if she should change, he should have told her to put on a pair of jeans...then his gaze wouldn't be glued, the way it was now, to her slender sun-browned legs.

He barely managed to stifle a groan. The right leg was stretched out as she pressed her foot to the accelerator; the left had relaxed as she concentrated on her driving, and it had fallen open with the knee resting against the car door.

She could have no *idea* what a seductive message she was sending out. It was enough to give a guy a heart attack.

It didn't help that he'd always been a leg man. And Willow Tyler's legs were the sexiest he'd ever seen.

He *itched* to touch...and found his gaze drawn again, hypnotically, to the sandaled foot arched over the accelerator. He wondered exactly where her most sensitive spot would be. Would it be those dainty toes? Or the paler skin of her instep? Or would it be—

"...I think here would be a good spot."

He jumped as if he'd been caught reading a novel in church. Was the woman a *mind reader?* His heart missed a beat as he saw that she was running a hand lightly over her left knee, the smooth, rounded knee lolling against the door.

She was inviting him to...?

Dazedly he stared at her.

She returned her hand to the wheel, and said, in a faintly mocking tone, "Haven't you seen enough?"

"Enough?"

She swung the car off the road and into a rest area. Apart from a camper parked at the far end, it was deserted.

What the heck did she have in mind?

She half turned in her seat and fixed her gray-green eyes on him. "Okay." Her tone was amused. "On a scale of one to ten, what's your assessment?"

"A ten." The word shot out before he could stop it. And anyway, why should he lie? She did have the most fabulous legs—

''Mmm. Myself, I'd have put it at a nine. I was overly cautious passing that cyclist just after we passed Miller's End, but they really give me the heebie-jeebies and...''

For a moment, he was lost. What was she talking about? And then...the penny dropped. She'd been referring to her *driving,* not to his lecherous appraisal of her legs.

''...and if you've seen enough, we'll go back. This rest area is as good a spot as any to turn. Besides—'' she ran a hand over her knee again ''—the sun's been glaring down on my leg and I feel the skin starting to burn.''

He sent up a silent prayer of thanks that he hadn't said anything to reveal he'd misunderstood her.

But he wasn't going to subject himself to another spell of sitting next her with nothing to do but feast his gaze on her glorious limbs.

He opened his door.

''Right,'' he said. ''We'll go back. But I'll drive.''

She didn't get out. She started, instead, to clamber over the gearbox from the driver's seat to the seat he'd vacated. And just before he slammed the passenger door behind him, he was treated to a view of inelegantly splayed legs; a view that threatened to raise his blood pressure to bursting point.

''Oh, you're back, Scott. Hi, there!''

Willow heard the melodic voice sing down from the stairwell as she and her employer crossed the front hall. Glancing up, she saw a woman come running down the stairs.

At sight of the stranger, Willow felt her breath catch. Scott Galbraith's sister-in-law was stunningly beautiful, with a terrific figure showcased in a clinging cotton-knit golf shirt and emerald-green shorts. Her cascade of curly hair was the color of black coffee; her eyes were even darker; and her lips were as red as a ripe hothouse tomato.

She positively vibrated with energy, and charisma oozed from her every pore.

"I've been chatting with Lizzie," she announced happily as she reached the foot of the stairs. "Scott, I'm *so* glad you've all come back to Summerhill, it's going to be *wonderful* having my nieces and nephew nearby."

Then focusing her eyes on Willow, she scanned her frankly while waiting to be introduced.

Willow felt her employer's firm hand on the small of her back.

"Camryn," he said, "this is the children's nanny, Willow Tyler. Ms. Tyler, my sister-in-law, Ms. Moffat—"

"Oh, don't be so formal, Scott!" Camryn Moffat stuck out her hand to Willow in a forthright manner. "'Ms. Moffat' makes me feel like some staid elderly aunt! I'm *Camryn.* And I'm going to call you Willow, if you don't mind."

Though Willow often felt intimidated by truly beautiful women, knowing how very ordinary she herself was, she didn't feel overwhelmed because this one was just so nice.

"I'd like that," Willow said. "If Dr. Galbraith doesn't mind."

He cleared his throat, before saying, somewhat stiffly, "No, Ms. Tyler. I don't mind."

"There." Camryn smiled. "That's settled then! And Willow's such a pretty name, I don't see why you can't use it, Scott, instead of 'Ms. Tyler.' Sometimes you can be such an old fuddy-duddy!''

Realizing that Camryn had put her employer on the spot, Willow flushed. But before she could even think what to say to smooth the moment, he said, even more stiffly,

''I just want to afford Ms. Tyler the respect her position warrants—''

''Oh, pooh!'' Camryn turned to Willow. ''Which would you prefer—Willow or Ms. Tyler?''

Willow felt her boss's eyes on her. And she sensed which answer he wanted to hear. But it wasn't the one she wanted to give. She said, honestly, ''I prefer Willow.''

She looked at him as she spoke, and she saw his eyelids flicker. She interpreted it as a sign of disapproval.

But before she had time to regret her quick decision, he said, ''I have no problem with that…however, let's level the playing field.'' His expression was mocking. ''From now on,'' he drawled, ''you'll call me Scott.''

After the couple left for the golf club, Willow went upstairs to see what her three charges were doing.

She checked on the younger two first and found them still asleep.

When she poked her head around Lizzie's door, she saw the eight-year-old sitting cross-legged on her bed, reading.

The child looked up when Willow entered, and with a scowl, immediately returned her attention to her book.

Willow crossed over to the bed. ''What are you reading?'' she asked in a friendly tone.

''A book.''

"Mmm, I can see that." Willow also saw crumpled wrapping paper on the floor. "A present from your aunt?"

"'Scuse me." Rolling away from her, Lizzie swung her feet onto the carpet, and got up. Nose in the air, she stalked to the door. "I have to go to the bathroom."

Seconds later, Willow heard the bathroom door crash shut.

The sound woke both Mikey and Amy. And as Mikey's fretty cries rent the air, followed by a yelled "Shut up!" from Amy, Willow braced herself for another pleasant afternoon.

Her employer didn't return home till late evening.

The children were in bed, asleep, and Mrs. Caird had retired to her apartment. Willow was sitting at the harvest table in the kitchen, sipping hot chocolate while she worked on the *New York Times* crossword in the *Sun* newspaper.

She'd just finished it when she heard a key in the back door lock. The door opened and Scott Galbraith came in.

When he saw her, he gave her his now-familiar faintly mocking smile.

"Hi, there," he said. *"Willow."*

She flushed. "I'm sorry your sister-in-law put you in an awkward situation. You don't have to call me... that."

"Ah, but I do. Camryn would have my head on a plate if I reverted to 'Ms. Tyler'." He looked at her mug. "What are you drinking?"

"Hot chocolate." She started to rise from her chair. "Can I make you some?"

He waved her down again. "Thanks, I had a late dinner at the club, drank too much coffee."

"How was your game?"

"Camryn beat the pants off me. She's a terrific golfer. Club champion of the ladies' division last year, and for the past several years, too. I haven't played much lately, but I'm looking forward to getting back into it."

He'd got a touch of the sun, Willow noticed. And the glow in his cheeks made his eyes seem more intense than ever.

"What does your sister-in-law do...other than play golf?"

"She has a boutique in Crestville. She designs most of the clothes herself. Her line's called CM Works. Are you familiar with it? Apparently one of her gowns was featured on the cover of *Vogue* in January."

"No." And if Camryn's designs were worthy of a *Vogue* cover, they certainly wouldn't be something Willow could afford! "But I'm not really up on fashion." She added, in a purposely offhand amused tone, "Plain-Jane, that's me."

His gaze sharpened. And lasered into her as if he was trying to determine whether that was a gibe. She could almost hear him asking himself if Ida Trent could *possibly* have been that indiscreet. But her own guileless expression apparently fooled him, because in a second or two she saw the suspicion clear from his eyes.

"Well," he said vaguely, "it takes all sorts..."

Suppressing a chuckle over his momentary discomfiture, she waited for him to leave.

But he seemed in no hurry. Leaning against the island in the center of the kitchen, he said, "So...how was your day? Making any headway with Lizzie?"

"I'm afraid not."

"How about Amy?"

"No."

He grimaced. "Look, I'm sorry—"

"No, *I'm* sorry. And I'm sorry I was so rude to you in Morganti's," she added in a rush. "I don't think I ever apologized for that. I didn't know the circumstances...but that's no excuse. Dr. Galbraith, I—"

"Scott."

"Dr. Galbraith, I find it hard to—"

"Call me Scott." He raised his eyebrows. "It's a simple word. One syllable." He nodded toward the newspaper section on the table, folded open. "Surely that's not beyond the scope of a young woman who can zip her way through the *New York Times* crossword?"

"It's not the *word* that's difficult, you know that! It's the fact that I'm the nanny, you're the boss."

"Can't you see me as...an ally, rather than a boss? Whatever battles you may have with the kids, I'm on *your* side. We have to present a united front. And if we're on a first-name basis, that would help make our position clear."

"It might. But...I can't call you...by anything other than Dr. Galbraith."

"That's final?"

"Yes."

"Then," he said with a melodramatic sigh, "Camryn's going to have my head on a platter."

She couldn't help smiling at that. "So you're going back to calling me—"

"Ms. Tyler." He pushed himself from the island. "And now, Ms. Tyler, I shall go to my study and allow you to enjoy the rest of your hot chocolate in peace."

As he exited, he called back, over his shoulder, "Good night, see you tomorrow."

"Good night, Dr. Galbraith."

The door swung shut and Willow relaxed muscles she hadn't even known she'd tensed. Whenever she was in the same room as Scott Galbraith, she found he affected her that way. Her muscles tensed—and her nerves hummed, her senses shivered. She was attracted to him, physically attracted to him. There was no point in denying it.

And she just couldn't call him by his first name. It would be far too...intimate.

Still...she was tempted to find out how it would sound on her tongue.

She inhaled a deep breath, and whispered: "Scott..."

But even as she pronounced his name she realized, to her dismay, that it came out sounding like a caress.

Willow had Thursday off.

And on Friday morning, she and the family breakfasted together, in the dining room.

After the meal was over, she told her charges to excuse themselves so she could take them upstairs to supervise their teeth-cleaning. But as she pushed to her feet, their father emerged from behind his newspaper.

"Hang on a minute, Ms. Tyler. Lizzie, you take Amy and Mikey upstairs. Ms. Tyler will follow shortly."

Willow sat down again as the children took off.

"So," her employer said, "how did you enjoy your break yesterday? What did you do last night?"

"Nothing too exciting. Mom made pizzas for supper and then I met up with a friend who has a little boy, Mark, and we took the boys to the park for a while.

Then Mark stayed at our house for a sleepover, and Brock took me dancing.''

''Brock?''

''Mark's dad.''

''He's on his own? Divorced? Or—''

''He's married but his wife—''

The door opened and Willow looked around.

''Excuse me, Dr. Galbraith.'' Mrs. Caird came in and put a package down in front of her employer. ''But this just arrived by courier and I thought it might be important.''

''Thank you.'' As the woman left, he set a hand on the package but kept his gaze on Willow. ''You were saying…?''

Was that a thread of disapproval in his tone? Had he jumped to the conclusion that she was involved in a deceitful relationship with a married man? The thought stung. Contrarily she decided not to enlighten him. Yet.

Wrinkling her nose, she said, ''Whatever it was, it's gone!'' And with a faint shrug of dismissal, added, ''I guess it couldn't have been important!''

His lips thinned.

Frowning, he tilted the package and set himself to studying the return address. When he looked up again, his expression was frosty.

''This is your uniform, Ms. Tyler.'' He dumped the package on the table between them. ''I suggest you start by wearing it for dinner tonight.''

''You're forgetting—you invited Camryn and her parents for dinner—''

''And you, Ms. Tyler, will join us. Do you have any objections to that?''

''No, I have no objections. It's just…normally, I don't join a family when they have dinner guests.''

"In this case, the guests *are* family." He exhaled an impatient sigh. "To repeat, you'll wear your new uniform for dinner, and then, as we agreed, you will wear it for a week whenever possible." He picked up his newspaper again. "Thank you, Ms. Tyler. That will be all."

Willow got to her feet. And as he buried his face behind the newspaper, she said lightly, "Oh, I've just remembered what I was going to say before Mrs. Caird came in. It was about Brock's wife, Jo. I was going to explain that she's my best friend but she doesn't like to dance, whereas Brock and I have been dance partners since high school and we go to Jazz Nights at the Grotto on a regular basis." She leaned across the table and scooped up the couriered package.

As she did, he looked up and she added, very pointedly, "With Jo's blessing, of course!"

Then she swung away from the table and sashayed out of the room.

She thought she heard him chuckle, even thought she heard a murmur that sounded like "Touché!" But she couldn't be sure...

Still, she wouldn't have put it past him. One thing she had already learned about Scott Galbraith...and it was something that she liked: the man had a sense of humor.

Fortunately she had one, too, for she certainly needed it later that day when she changed into her new uniform.

She stared aghast at her reflection in the bedroom mirror. Of all the colors in the spectrum, she decided, this shade of blue suited her least! It was way too harsh and totally drowned her out.

If she'd looked plain before, she looked positively sick now.

She'd dressed the children and settled them in Lizzie's room before going into her own room to change for dinner. As she made her way back to collect them, she wondered if they would notice what she was wearing.

They did.

And their reaction reinforced her own opinion.

"You look *yukky!*" Amy said, getting up from the carpet where she'd been building blocks with Mikey.

Lizzie set aside her book and raked her with a scathing glance before saying with a scornful sniff, "For once, Amy's right. You do *not* look good in that color!"

Mikey stared at her as if she'd suddenly grown two extra heads. "Not!" he said. "Not, not, *not!*"

Out of the mouths of babes.

Willow couldn't help laughing, and was about to say, "Thank you very much!" when she heard the doorbell ring.

Lizzie rolled off the bed. "They're here! Let's go!"

"Before we do," Willow said, "let's go through to the bathroom and give our hands a good scrub. And may I remind you all to be on your *very* best behavior. Try to make your father *proud* of you."

Ignoring her, Lizzie and Amy took off, jostling irritably in the doorway as each tried to beat the other to the bathroom. And once the hands were all washed and dried, Lizzie and Amy took off again, running helter-skelter to the landing and then clattering downstairs.

With Mikey in tow, Willow hurried after them, afraid the two would barrel rudely into the drawing room. But shyness overcame them at the last minute and they hung back when they reached the half-open door.

Willow finally caught up with them. And as Mikey tugged his hand from hers, she took in the pretty scene before her.

A handsome silver-haired couple were seated on a sofa angled out from the hearth, their faces turned toward Scott Galbraith and his sister-in-law, who were engaged in conversation over by the drinks table. Camryn was wearing an exquisite black cocktail dress; he was wearing a superbly cut dark suit.

And the intimacy between them was unmistakable.

Willow felt as if someone had reached into her chest and squeezed her heart, hard. They were indeed a beautiful pair...and they would be a perfect match.

In the moment before she knocked lightly on the door, she saw the silver-haired couple turn to each other and exchange satisfied smiles.

It was obvious to Willow that they were hearing echoes of exactly the same merry sound she was...

The peal of wedding bells.

CHAPTER FIVE

LIZZIE was the first to find her tongue.

"Hi, Grandma." Her black taffeta skirt rustled as she walked across the room. "Hi, Gramps."

"Lizzie!" The silver-haired lady held out her arms. "Darlings!" Her pale blue eyes shone as she welcomed her grandchildren. "Come and give your grandmother a huge hug!"

Once the grandparents had fussed over the children, Camryn's father lifted Mikey onto his knee, while Lizzie perched on an ottoman and Amy snuggled up on the sofa between her grandparents.

Willow hovered, and as Scott Galbraith came forward with his sister-in-law, she turned toward him for guidance.

At sight of her in the blue uniform, he did a double-take while Camryn stared at her, obviously taken aback, before pursing her lips.

The pair didn't say "Not, not, not!" as Mikey had done. They didn't have to; their expressions said it all.

Willow wished the floor would open up and she could dive into oblivion.

The doctor switched his attention to the couple on the sofa. "Elly, Craig, I'd like you to meet our new nanny, Ms. Tyler." He sent another glance Willow's way and when she saw the amusement shimmering in his eyes, she felt a stirring of outrage. "Ms. Tyler, these are the children's grandparents, Mr. and Mrs. Moffat."

Stifling an uncharacteristic urge to slap him, Willow

responded politely to his guests as they greeted her in an absent but friendly enough manner.

Her employer invited Willow, with a casual gesture, to sit on one of the occasional chairs, while he and Camryn moved over to a love seat by the hearth.

The Moffats were genuinely fond of the children, and the children, sensing this, chatted away quite happily and for once, didn't squabble among themselves.

After about fifteen minutes, Scott glanced at his watch and said, "Dinner should be ready around now. Lizzie, would you run through to the kitchen and ask Mrs. Caird if we should make our way to the dining room?"

Before Lizzie could get up from the ottoman, Amy shot to her feet. "I'll go, Dad!"

Lizzie scowled—and then to Willow's horror, shoved a leg out just as Amy raced past her. Amy tripped and went flying, ending up in a sprawl on the plush ivory carpet.

The child burst into tears, and Willow wasted no time in going to her aid.

For once Amy didn't push her away. But as Willow helped Amy to her feet, the redhead yelled, "You're a big pest, Lizzie Galbraith, and I hate you!"

Seeing his sister fall had upset Mikey and he started to scream. Shrilly. Nerve-scrapingly.

Willow felt her cheeks turn scarlet with embarrassment, and her spirits sank to a sickening low.

The evening was still in its infancy and already the children were letting her down. She darted a panicky look at her employer, and it was no great surprise to her to see that the amusement she'd spotted in his eyes earlier had vanished.

Dark irritation had taken its place.

* * *

"Thank you, Scott, for a lovely dinner. You've found a real treasure in Mrs. Caird. If you don't watch out I'll be stealing her from you," Elly added with a chuckle, as he helped her into the passenger seat of their silver luxury car.

"She's just teasing, Scott." Camryn ensconced herself in the back seat. "Bettina's a superb cook as you'll no doubt remember from your lunch at our place the other day!"

Her father started up the engine, and flicked down the windows. Camryn looked up at her brother-in-law.

"Scott, why on earth did you put that poor girl in a uniform? It's not like you to be so pretentious!"

"In the city," he began, only to be interrupted.

"Oh, pooh to the city!" Camryn waggled a red-tipped finger at him. "Get rid of it, Scott. Folks in this part of the world don't put their children's nannies in uniform. You're going to make the girl a laughing-stock!"

"Camryn!" Eleanor sounded scandalized. "Scott has every right to put the girl in uniform if he wants to. Personally I thought it added…tone. And let's face it, who ever looks at the hired help anyway. A nanny… well, she's just like part of the furniture."

"Part of the furniture indeed!" Craig shook his head. "Elly, sometimes I swear you're a bigger snob than your mother was!"

Scott laughed. And slapped the roof of the car with the flat of his hand. "Good night, folks." He stepped back as the car drew away. "See you again soon."

He stood there till the rear lights disappeared into the night, then he strolled back toward the house.

It was almost midnight, but the evening was still warm. The moon, at present, had hidden behind a cloud and the only light came from the sensor beams above the front door.

The children were asleep. He had let them stay up past their normal bedtime because after their little ker-fuffle in the sitting room before dinner, they'd behaved well enough. The girls had clung to Camryn, though, and had ignored Ms. Tyler, so shortly after dinner was over he'd told her she could take the rest of the evening off.

Ms. Tyler.

He shook his head wryly as he remembered his first sight of her in the blue uniform. For a moment he hadn't recognized her. And when he had, it was all he could do not to chuckle. But there was no doubt that she'd noticed the mirth in his eyes and he chuckled now, re-calling her outraged expression.

What a funny little duck she was.

And—he cocked his head as he heard the sound of an approaching vehicle—if he wasn't mistaken, the funny little duck was back.

He strolled out into the forecourt and when the car's headlights swept the front of the house, he waved her down.

She drew to a halt beside him.

In the car's interior light, he saw that she'd changed from her uniform into a white T-shirt and jeans.

"You want me to park here?" she asked through the open window.

"It's late, better not go into the garage and disturb Mrs. C."

He opened the door for her and with a murmured "Thanks," she swung herself up and out. He smelled chocolate on her breath—mingled with the soft femi-nine scent of the perfume she wore.

He caught her forearm as she would have made for the door. "Don't go in yet," he said. "I want to talk to you."

She stiffened under his touch. "About the children, of course." The moon chose that moment to sail out from behind the cloud and in its cold rays he saw that her cheeks had become flushed. "I'm sorry, Dr. Galbraith. I know they let you down—I know *I* let you down," she corrected herself. "I'd hoped that by now I'd have been able to reach Lizzie—"

"Ms. Tyler." His tone was gently chiding. "I'm not blaming you for Lizzie's meanness to her sister. And I told you at the beginning of the week that I didn't expect miracles. What I want to talk about is...your uniform."

"Oh. Do you have some problem with it?"

The stiffness had moved from her arm to her voice. And that was when he realized that he still held her forearm. He released her. "It was a mistake."

"A *mistake?*"

The moonlight made her T-shirt glow and its brightness acted like a magnet to his eyes. His gaze slid down, and it was only with difficulty that he dragged his attention up again from her small rounded breasts, which appeared to be quivering under the thin white fabric. "I want you to stop wearing it and go back to wearing your regular clothes."

"No."

"Why on earth not?"

"We agreed that I should wear the uniform whenever possible. And that's what I plan to do."

"Ms. Tyler." Frustratedly he dug his hands into his trouser pockets. "Do you enjoy being...difficult?"

"Dr. Galbraith." Her tone was sweeter than icing

sugar, and exaggeratedly patient. "I'm not trying to be difficult. I just believe it'll be greatly to *your* benefit if I continue to wear the uniform."

Alarm zinged through him. Surely she hadn't guessed the *real* reason he'd wanted her to wear a uniform?

"Of what possible benefit," he asked warily, "could it be to me?"

Her eyes had a mocking glitter. "When you asked me on my first day here what I thought of you, I said I figured you were under a lot of stress. Which you undoubtedly are. And according to the experts, one of the best things to relieve stress is laughter." She tilted back her head and somehow managed to look down her straight little nose at him as she added in a tone of unmistakable irony, "I certainly don't mind wearing a uniform and being the object of your laughter, Dr. Galbraith, if doing so will improve your health...and your *disposition*...in any way!"

She spun away from him, leaving him to stare after her as she stalked across the forecourt, up the front steps and through the open doorway.

And as his startled gaze followed her petite figure— her neat shoulders, her tiny waist, her pert behind, her long legs—even as he chuckled at her impudence, he was dismayed to feel a sudden stab of desire.

The same desire he'd felt on seeing her naked by the creek. Sweet and urgent. And *totally* inappropriate!

He rubbed a perplexed hand over his nape. Ms. Tyler was right about laughter being good for alleviating stress, but did she know that one of the *best* stress-relievers was sex?

He walked slowly up the steps, his thoughts drifting hither and thither, first to this and then to that...

But mainly to "that."

Sex.

Of which he hadn't had any for a couple of years; which was probably the reason he was now finding himself so easily aroused...and why he'd recently started having erotic and highly disturbing dreams.

Dreams about his children's nanny.

Dammit, if he was having erotic dreams, surely they should be about someone more...suitable. Someone in his social circle.

Camryn, for instance.

Now there was a woman who would make him a perfect mate. He latched desperately onto the thought.

Camryn was beautiful, she was intelligent, she was warm—and, according to the none-too-subtle hints her mother had tossed his way when her daughter was upstairs putting the children to bed—not only available but willing.

He should be thinking about getting married again. That way he could have sex whenever he wanted it. And that way, he could stop fantasizing about a certain funny little duck who, right now, would be upstairs in her room stripping off her plain white T-shirt and her hip-hugging blue jeans, stepping out of her panties, taking off her bra—

And there he was, back to "that" again. Imagining how "that" would be with an *entirely* inappropriate person.

He groaned, and with an effort, forced his thoughts back to Camryn: beautiful, charming Camryn, who was not only from an excellent family, but she was also a delightful companion and a ready-made mother for his unruly brood.

Squaring his shoulders, he made a decision.

First thing tomorrow, he would call her and invite

her out to dinner that evening. At a very elegant restaurant. And with the help of good wine, soft candlelight and romantic music, he would allow himself to be seduced into moving their longtime brother-in-law/sister-in-law relationship onto an entirely different footing.

When Willow brought her charges down for breakfast next morning, she found her employer already seated at the dining-room table. Sunshine streamed in through the window behind him, shimmering highlights into his black hair and shadowing his face as he perused his copy of the *Vancouver Sun.*

She'd been relieved last night when he hadn't asked her how she'd spent her time off. She couldn't have told him that directly after leaving Summerhill, she'd gone to place flowers on Chad's grave—and keeping that information from him would have been another lie between them, albeit a lie of omission. And he had made it plain that he prized honesty, hated deceit. If he ever found out…

But he never would. She was always very careful when she visited the Greenvale Burial Grounds; always made sure no one was around when she placed her flowers or pruned the rosebushes she'd planted so tearfully seven years ago.

He had looked up as she and the children came into the room. His eyes narrowed as he ran his gaze over the uniform, but he made no comment, instead just greeting her with a casual "Good morning, Ms. Tyler."

"Good morning, Dr. Galbraith."

The children ran over to him and he hugged them with a warm "Good morning, kids!"

The girls then took their places at the table, but

Mikey curled his fingers like pincers around the leather belt at his father's waist.

"Up, Dad!"

"No, Mikey, you'll have to sit in your high chair." He tried to extricate his son's fingers but when a wincing Mikey only tightened his grip, the doctor shot Willow an appealing glance.

"Ms. Tyler, would you...? I don't want to hurt him."

Willow crouched down beside the child.

"There's a trick to this." Smiling, she glanced up at her employer. "If you unlatch the baby finger, the others are easy." After she'd completed the exercise, she scooped Mikey up and shushing his protesting grumbles, strapped him into his high chair and set an empty bowl on his tray.

As she reached for the package of corn flakes on the sideboard, she kept her back to her employer so he wouldn't see the flush that had seeped to her cheeks after she'd glanced up at him. Their eyes had met for less than three seconds, but in that brief space she'd surprised a look of sexual awareness so blatant it had stopped her heart.

The man wanted her.

Oh, no, she *must* be wrong. He couldn't possibly want her. She was his plain-Jane nanny. Drab, and boring, with a face that would never launch a paper boat, far less a thousand ships. A man like Dr. Scott Galbraith couldn't possibly be interested in—

"Ms. Tyler, what on *earth* are you doing?"

The astonishment in his voice snatched her back to reality...and she noticed that Amy and Lizzie were giggling.

No wonder. Her face now went from pink to scarlet, for while she'd been struggling with her thoughts, her hands had apparently been busy. Too busy! She had poured half the packet of corn flakes, not into the empty bowl she had set on Mikey's tray but directly onto the tray itself. And Mikey was now sweeping the mounds of cereal off the tray and onto the carpet, chuckling with every delighted swipe.

"Oh, dear." Willow darted a horrified look at her employer.

And the expression in his eyes was so far removed from the expression she believed she'd seen there earlier, that she *knew* she must have imagined his sexual interest in her.

"I'm s-sorry," she sputtered. Gulping, she added, "I...my mind just wandered for a moment..." Her throat felt tight, her voice sounded thin. "I'll tidy—"

"Yes, you do that." He shoved his paper aside, lurched to his feet and fixed her with a dark scowl. "Now if you'll excuse me, I have a phone call to make."

He made for the door, but paused briefly on the way, his eyes shuttered as he turned to address her again.

"I'll be going out shortly, I'll be at the clinic with Dr. Black till late afternoon. And then," he continued with distinct emphasis on each word as if he were delivering a prepared and well-rehearsed speech, "I shall be taking Ms. Moffat out for dinner tonight. Could you please tell Mrs. Caird not to prepare any meals for me."

And leaving her staring after him blankly, he strode from the room, disapproval emanating from his every pore.

Willow took her charges to the creek midmorning, and once the trio had wriggled into their swimsuits they dashed into the lazily rippling water, making enough noise to frighten away every bird within a half-mile radius.

She seated herself on the grass with her back against a tree trunk, her eyes on the children but her thoughts on their father. What a strangely challenging expression had been in his eyes when he'd told her he was going out for dinner with his sister-in-law. And the odd tone he'd used...as if he'd been making a point.

But what that point was, she hadn't the foggiest idea.

Before she could puzzle it out, Amy tromped out of the water and plonked herself down on her towel.

The child plucked a blade of grass from the ground and nibbled it. She slanted Willow a surreptitious glance before looking away again quickly. Then, plucking out another blade, she fixed her gaze steadily on it and said, in a very quiet voice,

''I wonder why Lizzie's always so mean to me.''

Willow jerked her mind to sharp attention. It was the first time the child had initiated a conversation with her. Could this possibly be the breakthrough she'd hoped for?

''I don't know.'' She used the same quiet tone Amy had used. ''Why do *you* think she's mean to you?''

''She calls me a pest.''

''And I think that makes you sad.''

''She di'nt used to. Call me that.''

''So...when did it start?''

Amy lifted her head and fixed Willow with troubled blue eyes. ''It started after Sarah Anne left.''

''Sarah Anne?''

''She was our last nanny. The one that came after Belinda. Sarah Anne was *really* mean. She used to call Lizzie a pest, all the time! Well, 'cept when Dad was around. Then she was all nice and soft.''

So Sarah Anne had called Lizzie a pest. And Lizzie had stored up her anger...and it seemed as if she might now be transferring it to her sister. It would explain a lot.

"Was that why your dad let Sarah Anne go?" she asked gently. "He found out she was being nasty to Lizzie?"

"No. He di'nt know that. He let Sarah Anne go 'cos she wanted to sleep with him. That's what I heard cook say to Grandma Galbraith's chauffeur. I don't *know* why Sarah Anne would want to sleep with my dad. She had a really nice bedroom of her own." She squinted up at Willow. "Do *you* want to sleep in my dad's bed?"

Willow was thankful that Mikey chose that moment to scream, "Amy, come see fishies!" and Amy, easily diverted, jumped up and splashed into the water to join him—leaving Willow blinking in reaction to her innocent question.

Did she want to sleep in Scott Galbraith's bed?

If she were forced to answer that question, she'd have to say she'd never actually thought about *sleeping* in his bed. Admittedly his bed had featured in her dreams...but what he and she did together, in those dreams, had absolutely nothing to do with sleeping!

Late that afternoon, Scott parked his car across the road from the Greenvale Burial Grounds, and walked over to the cemetery's entrance.

He'd been at Summerhill for almost three weeks now, and had been putting this moment off, unwilling to face all the memories that would undoubtedly press down on him when he stood before his stepbrother's grave. But his conscience wouldn't permit him to delay the visit any longer. Bad enough that he'd let Chad down so badly in the past...

Nodding to a caretaker who was raking one of the paths, he strode along another of the paths, noting absently that most of the plots had a neglected air and that the lawns were sun-browned.

It was on a day such as this that they had buried Chad. It had been stiflingly hot, with not the slightest breeze to ruffle his father's graying hair, his weeping stepmother's black veil, his wife, Genevieve's, wide-brimmed black hat.

His heart twisted now as he reached Chad's grave. And for several moments he was so overcome with emotion that he didn't notice how well-tended the plot was. When he did, it was with a sense of surprise.

The granite headstone was spotlessly clean, unlike most of the others, which were white-stained with bird droppings. He raised his eyebrows at the sight of the two neatly pruned miniature rosebushes with their dainty yellow blossoms, and the sturdy glass vase with its colorful display of flowers.

Intrigued, and curious, he glanced around and saw that the only other cut flowers in sight were those at a fresh grave some distance away, which was smothered in wreaths.

He crouched down and inspected the pretty bouquet—white nicotiana and pink Michaelmas daisies and dark blue delphinium. They hadn't even *begun* to wilt. Someone must have placed them here recently.

But...who?

Even as he asked himself the question, the past snared his attention and he stood awhile, just thinking. Thinking of days gone by—days when he should have "been there" for Chad, days when he, to his lasting sorrow, had not.

Finally, expelling a weary sigh and wondering why he always found it so easy to forgive others for their shortcomings but impossible to forgive himself, he turned and made his way back along the narrow path.

The caretaker was still raking vigorously. But as Scott approached with an "Excuse me," he glanced up.

"Hi," he returned. "What can I do for you?"

"I wanted to ask about Chad Galbraith's plot." Scott indicated the grave's location with a wave of his hand. "Who's looking after it? The flowers...?"

"Got me on that one, I'm afraid."

"You've never seen anyone—"

"Uh-uh. Oh, somebody's tending it, but whoever it is—and my guess is, it's a woman—she's a bit of a mystery. Never seen hide nor hair of her. 'Course, I don't work evenings or weekends. She could be comin' in then. Whatever, that grave's the best tended in the park. Even in winter. If there ain't a bunch of 'mums for color, there's sprigs of holly. Or somethin'. Always somethin'."

Scott mulled this over as he returned to his car. And was still mulling it over as he set off for Crestville. A mystery woman. Who could she be? And why had she taken it upon herself to look after Chad's grave? The questions niggled and niggled at him as he drove up the highway.

But when he arrived at his destination, where he was welcomed warmly by his dinner date, he forgot all about Chad's grave and the mystery woman who tended it with such devotion, as he concentrated his attention on this *other* woman. The one who wasn't mysterious at all.

The beautiful and charming Camryn Moffat.

The lady he intended to make his wife.

CHAPTER SIX

"WHERE'S Dad?" Amy grumbled. "How come he's never home anymore, Lizzie?"

"Because he's working at the clinic now."

"I know where he goes in the daytime, but where does he go *after* he comes home from work and takes off again?"

"He's out with Aunt Camryn. He takes her out every night. I asked him and he told me. They go golfing or for dinner or *whatever!* Now finish cleaning your teeth and stop asking so many questions."

Later, as Willow tidied up the bathroom, she found herself recalling the girls' conversation, which she'd overheard as she was putting Mikey to bed. And when, shortly after, she made her way downstairs to the laundry room with a bundle of towels, their words stayed with her.

Since their father had started work at the clinic four days ago, the pattern of his life had changed. His days started early because he did rounds at the local hospital before going to the clinic, and he was usually gone before Willow and the children came down for breakfast. After work he came home and spent a half hour or so with Mikey and the girls, and then every evening he had gone out again.

During those four days, Willow had rarely seen him. And when she had, he'd been aloof. Formal. And, she sensed, faintly disapproving.

She had actually wondered if he went out in the evenings to avoid her. She'd assumed he'd gone back to the clinic to keep up with his paperwork. Apparently not.

Apparently he was courting his sister-in-law.

And that, Willow reflected wanly, as she went into the laundry room, was exactly what he *should* be doing. Camryn would be a wonderful mother to the children; and she'd make a perfect doctor's wife. She and Scott Galbraith were, after all, a perfect couple.

"Oh, rats!" she muttered. "Why do I always fall for the wrong—"

A brisk *rat-tat* on the laundry room door had her whirling around from the washing machine. And she saw the man of her thoughts standing in the doorway. Wearing a slate-blue jacket with a sand-colored shirt and matching slacks, he looked tanned and fit and as potentially dangerous as a charge of dynamite.

Nerves jangling, Willow turned back to close the lid of the washing machine, and took a couple of seconds to steady her racing heartbeats before turning again.

"What's wrong?" she asked.

"Why would you automatically think something's wrong?"

She resisted the urge to fold her arms defensively around herself. "I rarely see you, so I can't help thinking that if you come looking for me there must be a problem."

"There's no problem, Ms. Tyler. Not unless you choose to make it one."

"Make *what* one?"

"Let's go out to the patio." He seemed restless. "We can talk there. It's too damned hot in here."

She followed him out of the laundry room, along the hallway, through the dining room. He opened the screen door and stood aside to let her precede him to the garden.

As she brushed past him, she caught the faintest echo of his spicy cologne, and a hint of fresh male sweat. An erotic mixture. As she felt her senses tingle in response, she crossed to the middle of the patio to get away from him, and forced herself to focus on the silky richness of the night, and the star-spangled dark of the purple-velvet sky.

"I'll get us something cool to drink." His tone was brusque. "Hang on a minute. I'll be right back."

He went inside again, and after standing uncertainly for a moment, Willow walked onto the lawn and wandered down the garden.

The countryside was hushed, the only sound the muffled hoot of an owl in the forest, and the whisper of her crisp uniform skirt around her legs.

Her eyes gradually adjusted to the dark, and when she reached the giant oak tree in the middle of the lawn and looked up, her searching gaze soon located the square outline of the old tree house.

Chad's tree house.

She'd never been up there, of course—but Chad had told her about it.

He and she had been exchanging confidences, late on a dusky summer evening, as they lay together on a secluded grassy bank near the swimming hole.

She'd told him that her father had died when she was six, and her mother had brought her up alone. Chad had told her that when he was three, his father had walked out on his mother. But whereas Willow's mother hadn't remarried, Chad's mother, Anna, had met and married the widowed Galen Galbraith.

"I was eleven," Chad had reminisced, as he toyed

absently with Willow's soft hair. "And I thought it really cool to have a big brother. We hit it off right away. Actually he looked after me at Summerhill when our parents went on their honeymoon, and the very first thing he did was build me a tree house in the garden."

"He must have been a bit older than you then," she'd said.

"Yeah, he was twenty."

"He sounds like a nice person."

"He's the best."

Lost in the memories, Willow got a start when she heard her employer's voice from behind.

"Here," he said. "Lemonade."

He held out a glass.

And with a murmured "Thanks" she accepted it.

But before she could drink from it, he held out his own and clinking it to hers, murmured, "To new beginnings."

"New beginnings?" She hesitated, the glass half raised. "What kind of new beginnings?"

"As of tomorrow, you'll no longer be wearing that uniform."

"As I recall, we agreed we'd talk the matter over at the end of a week and—"

"After that week, you'd decide whether you found the uniform too…cumbersome, I believe was your word…for certain activities. Now, Ms. Tyler, I *defy* you to tell me you haven't found this to be the case. And I'm going to insist that you go back to wearing your regular clothes."

Willow opened her mouth to say her piece, but before she could, he said adamantly, "It was a mistake. Look, I don't want to get into a big argument about this—"

"You're not going to get any argument from me."

He did a double-take. "I don't understood. You seemed to be hell-bent on wearing it."

"I *was* hell-bent on wearing it…last week. Oh, I didn't want to at first…but when you obviously got such a charge out of seeing me in it, I decided I surely could put with its…cumbersomeness." Her mouth twisted in an ironic smile. "I thought it would be worth it."

In the silence between them, she could hear the rustle of leaves in a nearby shrub as a gentle breeze sighed past.

"But now," he said, "you don't?"

"I was mistaken. After your initial amusement, it was obvious you derived no further benefit from seeing me in the dress—in fact, your mood this past week—on the very rare occasions when you've been at home—has been dour to say the least. So that's why you'll get no argument from me. The uniform's history. The only reason I was wearing it," she added sparkily, "was in the hopes it might relieve some of your stress and put you in a better frame of mind. That hasn't happened, so I'll be more than happy to shove it in a drawer…where it can wait till the next nanny comes along!"

Willow wanted to snatch back her bold words but of course it was too late. What was it about this man that made her want to goad him; to poke a hole in his armor and find out what emotions he kept guarded deep inside?

Oh, she knew that where his children were concerned, his heart was nothing but mush. A mush of love and confusion. But of his other emotions she knew nothing. He was a mystery. She found him impossible to read…like trying to study a book written in a foreign language—

"Ms. Tyler...are you still with me?"

"Oh! Sorry...my mind wandered..."

"How very flattering! It's obvious," he teased, "your mother never told you that to keep a man's interest a woman should hang on his every word!"

"It's a long time," she shot back, "since keeping or even attracting any man's interest held any appeal for me!"

"Ah." He chuckled. "Ida Trent was right, then, when she intimated that you were a man-hater."

"I am *not* a man-hater! I'm sure Mrs. Trent didn't say that!"

"No," he admitted. "What she said was that the last thing you were looking for in your life was romance. But doesn't it boil down to the same thing?"

"No." She swallowed a mouthful of lemonade and felt the cold of it all the way to her stomach. "Hating men and not wanting romance are two entirely different things!"

"Doesn't every young woman, deep in her heart, long for romance? What soured you on love, Ms. Tyler? You're very young to be so...jaded."

"I'm not *jaded!*"

"Then why this reluctance to give your heart? You're shutting yourself off from the most wonderful thing in the world, that crazy feeling of being head over heels in—"

"I don't really want to talk about—"

"Ms. Tyler, have you ever swum in the ocean?"

Startled by the seemingly unrelated question, Willow hesitated, before saying warily, "No, I haven't."

"And have you ever seen a sunrise?"

"Well, of course, I've seen a sunrise! But why are you asking me these—"

"They say that in every person's lifetime, there are three things they should have done. Firstly, they should have swum in the ocean. Secondly, they should have seen a sunrise…"

"And thirdly?"

"Thirdly, they should have experienced what it's like to be in love. So, Ms. Tyler, my last question to you is have you ever been in love?"

The directness of the personal question shocked her and made her uncomfortable, but she wasn't about to let him know that. "I *believed* I was," she said. "Once."

"With your son's father."

"You promised, no more questions."

"That wasn't a question, Ms. Tyler. It was…an observation. So…you thought you were in love but it turned out to be—"

"Just teenage infatuation. Now," she went on quickly before he could comment, "am I to have a turn?"

"At what?"

"Asking questions."

"Shoot."

"Have *you* ever swum in the ocean?"

"Sure."

"And seen a sunrise?"

What little light there was in the night glinted on his black hair as he nodded. "Anyone who's had babies has seen more than their share of sunrises," he responded with amusement.

She chuckled. "Yes, I guess so."

Silence hummed between them again. She knew he was waiting for her to ask if he'd ever been in love, but she had gone just as far as she was going to. She now

regretted having let their conversation become as intimate as it had.

She turned away from him and started toward the
house. "I should be going in now, I'd like to check on
the children."

He fell into step beside her, and walked up the lawn
without speaking.

She was relieved that their conversation had come to
an end. But she was still intensely aware of him.

When they reached the patio, he opened the screen
door. She was so close to him, they were almost touch-
ing. And all of a sudden, her heart started to ache, filled
to overflowing with painful yearnings.

He stood back a little to let her precede him into the
dining room and when she brushed past him, she felt a
frisson of...something...pass between them. Phero-
mones, dancing in the air, fairies skimming back and
forth with tiny tantalizing invitations...

She'd never felt so weak, weak with longing to have
a man sweep her up into his arms.

In a daze, she walked with him into the front hall
and then she paused to say good-night before going upstairs. But before she could open her mouth, he took
the glass from her hand, startling her into looking up at
him.

His eyes had never seemed so blue, never seemed so
deep. She'd told the truth when she said she'd never
swum in the ocean but at this moment she thought she
knew what it must feel like to be drowning in it. And
she knew the same terror she'd have felt if her lungs
were filling with water. Was she really falling in love
with this man, this man who was so far out of her reach?

His voice dragged her up from the treacherous silky
waters even as her heart told her the answer.

"You didn't ask me the third question," he murmured, "but I'm going to give you the answer anyway. Yes, I have known what it is to fall head over heels for someone. I loved my wife, Genevieve, dearly. But nowhere," he added softly, "is it written that a man can give his heart only once. I'm not closing the door to falling in love again. In fact, Ms. Tyler, I'm already more than halfway there!"

As he got ready for bed a little later, Scott cursed under his breath. How could he have been so careless, and so selfishly self-indulgent, as to instigate such an intimate interchange with his children's nanny? When he'd gone looking for her after coming home, his only intention had been to tell her to stop wearing the uniform. It had all gone wrong and it had all been his fault. He'd been the one to take their conversation to a personal level. And that had been one gigantic mistake.

But he hadn't realized it—until he'd chanced to meet her gaze as he'd relieved her of the lemonade glass, and in her eyes he'd seen such innocence and such vulnerability he'd wanted to gather her into his arms and hold her close and swear he'd never let her come to any harm.

It was a feeling he had never had with his wife. Nor had he ever had it with Camryn. And that was because both women had always been perfectly able to look after themselves.

The two sisters had enjoyed a privileged upbringing, with every possible advantage. And as a result they had both become poised, accomplished, popular, successful and confident. More than anything, *confident*.

And while Ms. Tyler had lots of spunk, he sensed

that under the sparky exterior lay a cautious heart, a heart that was tender and easily hurt.

And the last thing he wanted to do was hurt her.

But in her gray-green eyes tonight he'd seen something more than the innocence and vulnerability. He'd seen bedazzlement and confusion—the expression of someone who was falling in love and didn't know what to do about it.

She'd looked, in a word, starstruck.

At the memory, he cursed again, roundly.

And his curses were aimed at Ida Trent. Hadn't he made a point of telling the woman to send him a nanny who wouldn't see him as a potential husband?

Willow Tyler, he was pretty sure, hadn't yet reached the stage of picturing herself walking down the aisle with him, but her imagination was going to get her there soon enough.

Unless he stopped her cold.

And that was why he'd told her, when he was speaking of love, that he was "already halfway there."

She would understand that he meant with Camryn.

He hadn't mentioned Camryn by name; how could he? He hadn't talked to his sister-in-law yet about marriage.

But the sooner the better. If anything was going to banish those dangerous stars from Ms. Tyler's luminous eyes, it would be the news that he was engaged to someone else.

Next day was Sunday, and Willow had the day off.

When she drove back to Summerhill that night, she found the household asleep. She herself headed straight for bed.

Next morning, she tossed the uniforms into the washing machine and in the afternoon took them off the line while the children were having their "quiet time," and pressed them before packing them into a plastic bag.

Mrs. Caird came into the laundry room while she was adding the white lace-up shoes to the bag.

The housekeeper saw what she was doing and said, "What are you going to do with these now, Willow?"

"I thought I'd put them in the Salvation Army bin in the mall," Willow said. "Unless you have a better idea."

"No, that sounds fine to me." The housekeeper lifted a bucket from the laundry tub. "You must be glad to get back to wearing your own clothes. Don't know what Dr. Galbraith was thinking about, to have you wear a silly uniform. It's not as if this is Buckingham Palace and you're going to be taking your charges to Hyde Park to be seen by all and sundry!"

Willow smiled. "I'm sure he had his reasons. But I must admit it feels good to be in my shorts and tank top again—especially in this heat!"

Mrs. Caird ran steaming water into the bucket. "Only one good thing about a uniform, it takes away the need to worry about what to wear on special occasions. Like this Friday, f'r instance. That'll be a dressy 'do.' What are you planning to wear?"

"Friday? What's happening on Friday?"

"Didn't the doctor mention it? Oh, maybe not, you were upstairs when the call came in and he left right after."

"What call?"

"His sister-in-law phoned him this morning, just before he left for the clinic. Apparently it's her parents' wedding anniversary on Friday, and Miss Moffat's going to throw a dinner party. So he—the doctor—told

me when he came off the phone that I needn't prepare
a meal on Friday night as you'd all be out.''

''But it's a family party. I won't be going.''

''That's not the impression I got. But of course,''
Mrs. Caird added, flicking the handle of her damp mop
from its metal clamp on the wall, ''I may be wrong.''

That evening, although Willow had meant to get to bed
early, she was still in the kitchen at midnight—struggling over the last corner of her crossword, which was
defeating her.

And she was *determined* to solve it.

She usually rattled it off in fifteen minutes. Tonight,
she was whisking through it as usual, till she'd hit this
wall and just couldn't get—

The back door opened and her pulse tripped over itself as Scott Galbraith came in. He looked so gorgeous
in an oyster-gray shirt and charcoal-gray slacks that if
she'd been standing, she feared she just might have
keeled over.

Fortunately she was seated, and was able to present
him with a bland questioning glance—while at the same
time unable to resist taking in other details of his ap-
pearance.

His black hair, she noted, was slightly—rakishly—
disarrayed.

And his eyes were as dark as the night outside, and
just as filled with secrets.

But one thing was no secret: he'd been out with
Camryn.

A smudge of her tomato-red lipstick adorned his
cheek.

Willow felt as if someone had run a rusty nail
through her heart.

"Hi," she said brightly, dragging her gaze from the red smear in the same ghoulish, reluctant way passing drivers dragged their eyes from a bloody car smash at the roadside. "Can I get you something? Hot chocolate? Or a—"

"No, thanks." He threw her a lopsided smile. "How come you're not in bed? You waiting up for me, *checking* up on me?"

"Hardly! I'm not your mother!"

He laughed. "No, that you're not! So...why *are* you up so late?"

"This dratted crossword. I was almost finished, but I got stuck. And that was an hour ago! It's *infuriating* me...but I just can't let it go!"

He crossed the room and stood by her chair. "Let's have a look." Casually he rested a hand on her shoulder.

Her breath caught...and she barely managed to keep her shoulder from stiffening under his light touch.

"Ah," he said, "I see where you've gone off track. This is the *New York Times* crossword so it's U.S. spelling. You've got defence here, it should be defense. And that makes this not *c i r e* but *s i r e*..." He took the pencil from her hand, and leaning over the table, changed the *c* to an *s*. "And that," he said, "would make this word—"

"Desire!"

"Right," he murmured. "Desire it is."

He gave back the pencil, and she expected him to move away. He didn't.

Uncomfortably aware that he was watching her, she slotted in the remaining missing letters to complete the crossword. And the moment she'd finished, she pushed the paper aside and got to her feet. Since he didn't seem disposed to leave, then she would. Being alone with him was as tantalizing as being alone in a chocolate factory—who knew what she might be silly enough to do in the face of such temptation!

"Thanks for your help," she said, and stepping toward the door added over her shoulder, "Good night, Dr. Galbraith."

"Hang on a minute…"

She stopped in the doorway, and turned around.

He had come after her. And was too close for comfort. "I just wanted to ask you," he said, "if Mrs. C. mentioned that we'll be going to the Moffats's on Friday night?"

"She said you and the children had been invited to a party to celebrate your in-laws' anniversary."

"That's right. Dinner's at seven, we'll leave here around five-thirty."

"That's late for the children. I'll make sure they all have a nap in the afternoon then I'll give them a snack around four and have them dressed and ready for you by five-thirty."

"You'll get yourself ready, too, Ms. Tyler."

"You…want me to come with you? But Camryn's so good with the children, you won't need me—"

"My sister-in-law's going to have her hands full— she's invited forty guests, her hostessing duties won't leave her much time to spare for Mikey and the girls and she specifically asked that I bring you. So there you have it, Ms. Tyler. Any questions?"

"No." None that she would care to ask him! But she was already asking herself the age-old one: What on earth was she going to wear? She certainly had nothing in her wardrobe that was suitable for a party at the Moffats's.

"Oh, one last thing," he said. "Camryn wants to treat the girls to new outfits for the 'do.' She says she has some specially attractive dresses in her boutique right now. So could I ask you to drive Amy and Lizzie there tomorrow afternoon? I'll make a point of being home from the clinic by one to keep an eye on Mikey."

"Wouldn't you like to take the girls yourself, and leave Mikey with me?"

"Camryn said shopping for dresses is a 'girl thing'— and besides, it might give Lizzie a chance to soften her attitude to you. I have to tell you, I'm beginning to lose patience with her. I've been considering, lately, whether I should take her aside and give her a good talking to—"

"No amount of talking can make her accept me— and it might only increase her hostility if you intervened."

He grimaced. "I guess you're right."

"If she and I are to be friends, I have to win her over by myself. I'm sure she believes that if she continues to challenge me at every turn, I'll eventually hand in my notice. It's not going to happen. And once she realizes that I'm here for the duration—or at least till you no longer require my services and let me go—"

"*That* is not going to happen! Don't even *talk* about giving in your notice. The very thought of having to start over again with another nanny makes me shudder! Now," he added, "it's time you were getting off to bed."

"Yes, it's late. Good night, Dr. Galbraith."

But as she turned to leave, she tripped over her own feet. And if he hadn't grabbed her quickly by the shoulders she'd have landed with a splat on the floor.

Breathlessly she looked up at him. "Thanks!"

Their eyes met and his gaze was so intense, it caused a shock of awareness to rocket through her. Stunning her. For the longest moment, they stood there together, their eyes locked...and she felt again the sensation of drowning in the depths of a silky deep blue pool.

Finally he blinked. Twice. And released her.

"You okay?" he asked, his voice husky.

"Yes, sorry about that, clumsy of me." Embarrassedly she murmured another "Good night" and then fled.

Her bedroom, when she reached it, was like a haven. She swung the door shut behind her, and running across the carpet, threw herself down on the bed. Rolling onto her back, she stared with stark dismay at the ceiling.

She had seen it *again*, just as she'd seen it before. But last time, she thought she'd been mistaken. Dr. Scott Galbraith surely couldn't want her, mousy little her.

But he did. Oh, yes, he did.

The desire in his eyes had been as clear as the word had been on the page, when he'd printed it shortly before.

CHAPTER SEVEN

HANNAH HO, the medical clinic's receptionist, showed Scott's final patient of the morning into his office at noon.

Scott finished scribbling a few notes in the file of the previous patient, before turning his attention to the middle-aged woman who had taken the seat by his desk.

"Mrs. Roberts. How are you today?"

"I feel just awful." She snuffled, and taking a tissue from her bag, blew her nose loudly. "My head feels all plugged up and my throat's sore, and..."

Scott listened while she talked, and then after asking her a few questions, he examined her thoroughly. Concluding that she had nothing more nor less than a case of the common cold, he told her so.

She sneezed into a second tissue. "Could you give me a prescription?" Her voice was thick.

"I could, Mrs. Roberts...but you know what? You're going to get better if you take medicine...but I guarantee you're going to get better even if you don't—"

"I saw this medicine advertised on TV that would make me feel *ever* so much better!"

"Most of the cold remedies you see advertised on TV are useless. The only people who feel better from them are the drug companies when they tally up their enormous profits!"

She grimaced. "That's what my hubby always says. He's great believer in letting nature take its course."

"He sounds like a man after my own heart! Why

99

don't we give that a try,'' he said coaxingly. ''And if you're not feeling a bit better by Monday, come back and see me again. In the meantime, I'll tell you a few things you can do on your own to help alleviate the sore throat.''

After she'd gone, he rolled his chair back and stretched out his arms to ease tightened muscles. It was the first time that morning that he'd had a moment to relax...or to think about anything except his work. But now, as he stared out his office window, he found himself thinking about Camryn.

Last night he'd taken her to a dinner/dance at the country club. Afterward, he'd driven her home but had declined her offer of a nightcap, so they'd parted company at her front door. He'd embraced her lightly and she'd planted a kiss on his cheek. She'd been lovely and feminine and scented; and in no apparent hurry to go in. So why hadn't he done what she'd surely expected him to do? Why hadn't he pulled her close and claimed her lips in a passionate kiss that would have brought their relationship to a different level?

He compressed his mouth grimly as he answered his own question. He hadn't taken advantage of the moment because what he felt for Camryn Moffat was what he'd always felt for his wife's sister: pure and simply, brotherly affection.

And what did he feel for his plain-Jane nanny? What was there about that girl that fascinated him so? When he'd looked into her eyes last night after she'd tripped, he'd been...lost. *Totally* lost...and what he'd felt for her then had certainly not been brotherly affection. It had been desire.

And he didn't know how to handle it.

Neither, obviously, did she. She'd taken off like a scalded mouse as soon as he'd released her.

And the situation he found himself in was untenable. He wanted her...but he didn't *want* to want her!

Camryn was the right woman for him; and the affection he felt for her—surely it would deepen to love come time? Perhaps the reason he didn't desire her physically was that she had, for so long, been his sister-in-law and he'd seen her as only a friend. But things were different now. And all he had to do was get used to that idea. Which he would.

In the meantime, he'd give Ms. Tyler a cold, hard look and try to figure out what it was about her that tantalized him so. And once he'd pinned it down, whatever it was, he'd dissect it ruthlessly till it lost its seductive powers over him, and then he'd be able to focus all his attention where it belonged: on courting Camryn.

"I wanna see Aunt Camryn, too!"

Willow scooped Mikey up out of his high chair and gave him a hug. "I know, sweetie. Next time, you will. But today's a girls' shopping outing."

"Besides," Amy said, dipping her spoon into her plate of strawberry mousse, "you're a lucky boy 'cos Dad's going to look after you, and we *hardly* ever get to see him."

"That's because he's a busy doctor." Lizzie gave a supercilious sniff. "Who do you think would pay for our house and everything else if we didn't have a dad to go out to work?"

"Willow's little boy doesn't have a dad," Amy pointed out. "And he has a house. Why doesn't Jamie have a dad, Willow?"

As Willow wondered how best to answer Amy's

question, she sensed someone watching her. Turning, she saw Scott Galbraith standing in the dining-room doorway. He was staring at her in a hard, assessing way that gave her goose bumps.

Why was he...*examining* her like that? Was he remembering last night? Was he wondering if she'd faked that stumble so she'd end up in his arms? At the notion, she felt her stomach give a leaden twist. He'd wanted a nanny who wasn't man mad; did he now believe that that's what she was? Did he now believe he'd made a mistake in hiring her? She prayed not. She needed this job; and she desperately wanted to keep it.

Struggling to ward off a feeling of apprehension, she said, "Oh, hi. I was about to take Mikey upstairs and get him ready for his nap."

"I'll take him." He walked across the dining room, and held out his arms for his son.

She lowered her eyes, kept them fixed on Mikey during the exchange, but when her employer's fingertips brushed her wrists she felt a whisper of electricity pass between them; and unable to help herself, she darted a glance at him.

He was frowning.

And he stepped back abruptly.

But even as tension clenched Willow's stomach into a knot, Amy finished her dessert and said casually, "I was asking Willow where Jamie's Dad is. Where is he, Willow?"

Her father said, "Don't ask personal questions, Amy. You know it's rude."

"Sorry," Amy mumbled. "I didn't know it was personal and I didn't know it would be rude to ask about Jamie."

"That's all right," Willow said. "I don't mind your

asking. Jamie's dad died several months before Jamie was born.''

For a moment, silence reigned in the room. It was broken, unexpectedly, by Lizzie.

"Excuse me," she said roughly, pushing her plate aside, the strawberry mousse half-uneaten. She lurched up from her seat. "I'm going to clean my teeth."

She ran from the room, leaving Willow staring after her in surprise. Lizzie *loved* strawberry mousse. Besides which, she was never in any hurry to clean her teeth. Like most children, she had to be prodded into it. Usually, but not, for some unknown reason, today. The child was as much a mystery to Willow as her father was!

"Let's go upstairs, Amy." She pulled out Amy's chair. "We'll get your teeth cleaned, too, then we'll be on our way."

Amy ran off, and the doctor swung Mikey up onto his shoulders, falling into step beside Willow as she walked out to the hall.

On their way upstairs, he said quietly, "You didn't tell me...about Jamie's father."

Willow experienced the shrill clang of alarm she always felt when he spoke about Chad—although, of course, *he* didn't know it was his stepbrother they were discussing.

"I told you," she said in a tone that indicated she had no interest in further discussing the matter, "that my son's father was no longer in the picture."

"Yes, but I had no idea you'd had to go through your pregnancy without him. That must have been hard for you—"

"I didn't think there was any need to go into detail," she broke in firmly. And realizing that she had, here, a perfect opening to let him know, albeit subtly, that if he suspected she'd tripped deliberately the night before, he was wrong, she added, ''What you and I have is a strictly *business* relationship. And as I've mentioned to you before, I like to keep my business life *completely* separate from my personal life. In my own mind, I see a distinct line between the two and it's a line I don't wish to cross.''

While she was talking they'd reached the top of the stairs. And the girls were just coming out of the bathroom.

Before he could make any response, Amy called, ''We're almost ready!'' and she and Lizzie crossed to their bedrooms, Amy skipping, Lizzie flouncing along behind in a disdainful way that didn't bode well for their upcoming outing. ''I just have to get my dolls,'' Amy called as she disappeared from sight, ''and Lizzie has to get her book.''

''You won't forget to clean Mikey's teeth?'' Willow said to the man standing beside her.

''No, I won't forget to clean Mikey's teeth—''

''And don't give him anything else to drink, not before his nap.''

''No, I won't give him anything else to drink, not before his nap.''

''And after his nap, he likes milk and a cookie.''

''And after his nap, he likes milk and a cookie.''

She'd avoided looking at him as she gave the instructions, but something in his tone made her flash him a sharp glance. He had sounded…teasing.

And yes, there was a definite twinkle in his eyes.

He was *laughing* at her.

''What's wrong?'' she asked. ''What have I said to amuse you now?''

He chuckled. "I don't know. You just make me laugh."

He had the most disarming smile. And when he looked at her like that, as if he just enjoyed *being* with her, it made her melt like chocolate in a child's hot little hand. But it also made her wonder why on earth he'd inflicted such an icily assessing glare on her earlier.

Lizzie and her sister emerged from their rooms, and Willow knew she didn't have time to wonder about him now.

It was time to be on their way; she didn't want to keep Camryn waiting.

But she did say to him before taking her leave, and with a completely deadpan expression on her face, "Isn't that wonderful, I'm so glad I continue to be a source of amusement, even without the blue uniform. If this keeps up, Dr. Galbraith, you'll soon be totally stress-free. And we shall all be the fortunate beneficiaries of your resulting consistently cheerful disposition!"

Scott stood at Mikey's bedroom window and watched Ms. Tyler escort Amy and Lizzie across the forecourt to her car.

She had been so serious as she gave him the instructions for Mikey, as if each little item were a matter of life and death. He couldn't help but laugh. And then, when she'd teased him in return, without as much as a twitch of her lips to indicate that she was having fun at his expense, he'd felt a stab of shame that he'd scrutinized her so ruthlessly when he'd spied on her from the dining-room doorway. He cursed under his breath now, as he recalled the bewilderment in her eyes when she'd caught him giving her that cold once-over—

"Drink, Dad."

He winced as Mikey tugged his hair. "Ouch, you little rascal! No, no drink! You'll have your milk later. Now let's get your teeth cleaned and put you down for your nap."

Ms. Tyler, he noticed, had settled the girls in the back seat of the car and was walking around the vehicle. She had just reached the driver's door when the housekeeper appeared from the direction of the garage. She had a young man with her. Tall, blond, good-looking, the stranger was wearing faded jeans and a black muscle shirt.

When Mrs. Caird called, "Willow!" the nanny turned, her hand on the door handle.

The bedroom window was open, so he could hear their voices—couldn't actually hear what was said, but it was obvious that the housekeeper was introducing the nanny and the young man. Or maybe not. It seemed—from their interactions—as if the two already knew each other.

They all three chatted briefly, and then Mrs. Caird and her companion moved away and walked toward the house.

Scott expected that Ms. Tyler would then jump into the car and be on her way. Instead, to his surprise, she stood staring after the young man and on her face was an expression of dismay—no, more than dismay, an expression of horror. She looked appalled. And she looked frightened.

As he watched, puzzled, she put a hand against the car as if to steady herself, and pressed the fingertips of the other hand against her mouth, as if to keep back a cry.

What the *devil* was going on?

But even as he asked himself the question, Amy

rapped sharply on the car window and he saw the nanny
start.

Even from this distance, he could see her gather herself together. When she turned to Amy, she was smiling.

And a few seconds later she was in the car and the
car was wending its way down the driveway.

He was left lost in a sea of questions to which he
was well aware he might never know the answer.

And the answer, of course, was none of his business
anyway.

"So, Lizzie, the choice is yours." Camryn smiled at her
niece. "The buttercup-yellow or the periwinkle-blue.
Which is it to be?"

"Dunno." Lizzie glanced at Amy, who was pirou-
etting in front of a three-way mirror, as dainty as an elf
in the leaf-green dress she'd chosen.

"Which one do *you* prefer, Willow?" Camryn asked.

Amy danced over. "I like the yellow one best."

"I think I do, too," Willow murmured. "The color's
wonderful with your hair, Lizzie."

Camryn took Amy by the hand. "While your sister's
making up her mind, let's find you a fancy pair of
socks."

They moved to another part of the boutique, and
while Willow looked on, Lizzie took first one dress and
then the other, holding each in front of her at the three-
way mirror.

"Why don't you try them both on again?" Willow
suggested.

"I don't need to." Lizzie's tone was terse. "I can
remember what they looked like."

Willow almost shot back a sarcastic "Sorreeee!"
Instead she leaned back against the counter behind her,

feeling suddenly weary. She still felt drained after the shock of learning that Mrs. Caird's foster son was in town. She'd barely been able to hide her horror as she and the housekeeper and Chad's old friend had chatted in the forecourt. But once they'd left, she'd felt faint, and terrified. Then Amy had rapped on the car window and brought her back to her senses. And she'd forcibly pushed all her worries to the back of her mind, and was doing a good job of keeping them there, for the time being.

It would have helped if Lizzie hadn't been bent on ruining their outing. She'd slumped in the car all the way to Crestville, and had shown little interest in looking at the dresses Camryn had brought out for her, although she'd finally deigned to try on a couple. Willow suspected she really liked both dresses, but was determined not to show it.

Now as Willow glanced over at Camryn and Amy who were having a grand old time looking at socks, Willow found herself wondering if and when Lizzie ever had a grand old time. Certainly never when Willow was around to see it; then she was usually dour and uncooperative...and often quite rude. On more than one occasion, Willow had been tempted to smack the child's little bottom, but she knew in her heart that she never would. What the child needed was not a spanking; what she needed was love and a feeling of security.

And Willow was determined to give her both.

Sometimes, though, she wondered if she was fighting a losing battle. School would be going in next week, and Lizzie would be away all day. Their time together would be shorter, the opportunities to win her over would be fewer.

Heaving out a sigh, Willow drew her attention from

Camryn and Amy, and returned it to Lizzie...only to find that the little girl was watching her...staring at her with an oddly defensive expression in her eyes, one that Willow had never seen there before. What was the child going to come out with now? What little nastiness had she thought up to further ruin the outing?

Willow pushed herself from the counter and straightened to her full height, before addressing Lizzie in a quiet voice. "What is it, Lizzie? Don't keep it all bottled up. Spit it out. You'll feel better if you do."

Lizzie clamped her forearms over her waist. And then after a pause that seemed endless to Willow, said, in a voice even lower than Willow's had been, so low it was almost a whisper, "When are we going to get to meet your little boy?"

Willow couldn't have been more astonished if the child had asked when she was going to get to meet the Dalai Lama.

"Jamie?" she asked. "You want to meet *Jamie?"*

Lizzie pressed her lips together. And nodded.

"Why, sweetie? Is there some special reason?"

For heaven's sake, Willow thought...are those tears in the child's eyes? But even as she asked herself if it could possibly be, and if so, why, Lizzie turned her back on her and said, in a muffled voice, *"Can* we...meet him?"

"Yes, of course. I'll talk to your father. Actually he already suggested to me a while ago that it would be a good idea for you and Amy to meet Jamie before school went in. How about we do something together on Saturday?"

Again, the child nodded. Then in a muffled voice, she said, "You like the yellow dress best?"

"Yes, they're both lovely but the yellow one is special."

Fully expecting that Lizzie would then be her usual contrary self and say, "Then I'll take the blue!" Willow got a shock when the child scooped up the yellow dress, and walked away across the store.

And as Willow watched, stunned, the little girl handed the dress to her aunt. "I've decided, Aunt Camryn. This is the one I want. Thank you very much."

Totally unaware of the little drama that had been going on, Camryn smiled at Willow, who was still trying to come to grips with what had happened.

"And now, Willow, we have to find a dress for you."

Willow hastily said, "Oh, no, Camryn, I can't possibly afford to shop here!"

"Perhaps not normally," Camryn said. "But I have a lovely dress that was custom-made for a client's trousseau but the wedding was called off and I told the client I'd try to sell it for her. I assure you the price will fit your pocketbook—no," she said firmly as Willow attempted to protest again, "you must at least try it on. And you'd be doing me a favor by taking it off my hands. It's not a size or style that would suit any of my regular clients, but since you're petite I think it's going to be perfect on you. Now just let me find a pair of socks for Lizzie, and we'll go through to the back and you can try the dress on."

Scott was playing ball with Mikey in the backyard when he heard the car purring up the driveway.

He glanced at his watch. Seven-thirty. He'd have expected them earlier if Camryn hadn't phoned to say that she was taking the children and the nanny out for dinner.

"We've all had a wonderful time shopping," she'd said enthusiastically. "Just wonderful."

"And you managed to kit out the girls for Friday night?"

"They're all set. But you mustn't ask to see their dresses, they want it to be a surprise."

"A surprise it shall be, then," he'd said, amused. "And thanks, Camryn. It was kind of you."

"What's the point of having a boutique if I can't treat my favorite people to outfits once in a while! Scott, I have to run, our table's ready. Bye…"

So here they were, home at last.

"Let's go inside, buster." Scott scooped the big blue ball and rolled it under the picnic table. "Your sisters are home."

"Willow's home!" Mikey cried excitedly, taking off toward the back door as fast as his sturdy legs would carry him. "Willow, Willow, Willow!"

Scott strolled after him, trying to tamp down his own feelings of anticipation, the tingles of excitement dancing through his veins. He'd expected to enjoy his afternoon off, alone in the house with Mikey who had slept for the best part of two hours and given him all the solitude he'd thought he wanted. But instead of savoring the peace and quiet, he'd been unable to settle. The house had been too quiet, too…*lonely*. Without Ms. Tyler's presence, Summerhill felt like the empty shell it had been when he and the children had first taken up residence.

But that would all change, he assured himself as he followed Mikey's thudding little footsteps along the corridor to the front hall. Once he married Camryn and brought his bride to Summerhill, he'd never be lonely again.

Camryn. *She* was the one who should excite him.

What was he thinking, allowing himself to be drawn to his children's nanny like a desperately cold moth to a softly glowing flame? He must be out of his mind.

He stopped abruptly in the corridor, and stood there, hearing the front door burst open, hearing the girls bound into the entry, hearing Mikey scream, "Willow, Willow!" and hearing Ms. Tyler's sweet voice greeting the child.

"We brought you a present, Mikey!"

"It's a spinning top!" Amy said eagerly.

"And it's got every color in the rainbow," Lizzie added. "I can't wait to show you! It spins so fast it'll make your own head spin just watching it—"

"And it sings," Ms. Tyler said, with a laugh. "It really sings. Let's go upstairs, children. First of all, we must put away the dresses—"

"We're going to hide them." Amy giggled. "We don't want Dad to see them till Friday, it's to be a surprise…"

"Where's your father, Mikey?"

Scott didn't catch what his son said, but apparently it had satisfied the nanny for he then heard the sound of the group ascending the stairs, the children running, Ms. Tyler saying, "Give me your hand, Mikey."

And then in a few seconds, he heard them all laughing and the children talking over each other as they crossed the landing and went into one of the bedrooms. Then he heard a door slam. Followed by silence.

He shoved his hands into his pockets, and scowling, he picked up his step again and made his way through to the sitting room. Feeling frustrated and impatient and—yes, he admitted it—left out, he crossed to the liquor cabinet and poured himself a nip of Scotch. He walked over to the window, and with the heavy crystal glass in his hand, stood there, staring moodily out, lost in his thoughts.

He was still standing there fifteen minutes later, the drink barely touched, when he heard Ms. Tyler's voice come tentatively to him from the doorway.

"Dr. Galbraith," she murmured, "may I talk to you?"

CHAPTER EIGHT

SCOTT gulped down a mouthful of his drink. And felt it burning right to his stomach as he turned around.

She—Ms. Tyler, this burr under his skin—was hovering just inside the door, and in a fresh white shirt and neatly pressed black jeans, she looked as prim as Mary Poppins. Or she *should* have done, and *might* have done, if her cheeks hadn't been flushed and her eyes hadn't been sparky-bright and her silky hair hadn't been sun-streaked as summer itself.

Suppressing a groan, he gulped down the last of his drink and set the glass on the top of the nearest bookshelf.

"Yes." He sounded gruff. Impatient. But he was impatient only with himself, though of course she wasn't to know that. "What is it?"

Her eyes had dulled. She stood rebuked—for she knew not what. And he felt like a heel.

"I had a chat with Lizzie," she said. "I'm not sure what brought it on but she told me she'd like to meet my son."

"Lizzie's coming around, you think?"

"I don't know. But…I sense there might be a little chink in her armor."

"Well, you know you don't have to ask me if Jamie can come here. I told you a while ago that I'd like Amy and Lizzie to meet him before the school term started, but you nixed the idea."

"Yes, I remember. And I still don't want him to

come here. What I thought was—if you don't mind—I might take the children to my mother's tomorrow afternoon.''

"But that's your day off—"

"I'll be spending it with Jamie anyway and it'll be fun for him, to have Mikey and the girls to play with. What I thought was, I'd go home as usual in the morning, but I'd come back for the children after they have their quiet time. And maybe they'd like to stay at my mom's for dinner. If you don't mind.''

"Of course not.''

"Then that's settled. Thank you, Dr. Galbraith. That's all I wanted to ask.'' She made to turn away, but he said,

"Hang on a sec.''

She waited, her expression questioning.

"I was just wondering…who was that lad visiting Mrs. Caird this afternoon? I saw the three of you talking, just before you left for Crestville.''

At his question, her cheeks paled. And a shutter came down over the questioning expression in her eyes. She swallowed, before answering. But when she answered, her voice was very steady.

"He's Daniel, Mrs. Caird's foster son.''

"Ah. Does Daniel live in the area?''

"No, he lives in Toronto. He's just visiting for a few days.''

"You knew him before?''

"Not really. He was ahead of me in school. By a couple of years.''

"So you didn't know him well.''

"No.'' The reply was clipped, as her previous replies had been. And her stiff attitude told him plainly that she wanted no part of this conversation.

He himself wanted to press for more information, wanted to find out what it was about this Daniel that had frightened her. But he was pretty sure she wasn't about to spill out any answers so he decided to leave it…for the time being.

"I want you to know," he said, "that if you ever have any problems, any problems at all that you can't cope with, you're to come to me and I'll help if I possibly can. Okay?"

For a fraction of a second, he thought she was going to cry. Her lower lip certainly trembled…but she got herself under control right away. "Thank you," she said, all at once as prim and crisp as her outfit—and her eyes had a spark again, a spark of independence. "But I don't have any problems, Dr. Galbraith…at least none that I can't handle."

"Good." He smiled in a bland and indulgent way that he hoped would assure her it hadn't even wildly occurred to him that such a capable young woman as she, with such a well-ordered life, could ever have any troubling problems.

Gesturing with an open hand toward the door, he added, "Then that's all for now, Ms. Tyler. You may go back upstairs and tend to your charges."

Willow stood at her bedroom window, staring out over the pitch-black landscape. She shivered, even though the room still held the heat of the day. Why was it that in the night hours, every worry seemed intensified, every problem insurmountable?

She'd been trying for ages to get to sleep, but in vain. She couldn't stop thinking about Daniel. What if he should find out that she had a six-year-old son? He would remember that she and Chad had been lovers seven years ago; it wouldn't need the brain of an Einstein to figure out that Chad must be Jamie's father. And wouldn't Daniel then mention this to his foster mother, since Mrs. Caird was now working for Chad's stepbrother and living at Summerhill?

Willow sighed, and fluffing her nightie away from her heated body, asked herself what would happen then. Would Mrs. Caird tell Dr. Galbraith that his children's nanny was actually the mother of his stepbrother's child?

How would he feel about her then, knowing she'd been so deceitful? Oh, she hadn't actually lied to him, but wasn't lying by omission just as bad as telling an outright untruth?

What would he do if he found out?

First off, he'd fire her. No doubt about that. He wouldn't want her around his children, not when she was so deceitful.

But he'd loved Chad. So he would want Jamie. He would want to take Jamie into the bosom of the Galbraith family.

She would fight him, of course.

But she'd be without a job again, and with his resources and background, how could she win? She might have had a slim chance if he'd been single, but he was going to marry Camryn. The couple would be able to offer Jamie the kind of family life any judge would applaud.

She could take Jamie and run, of course. But that would break her mother's heart.

So she was trapped. Trapped at Summerhill, with the walls starting to close in around her.

She had asked Mrs. Caird's foster son—in a deliberately casual tone—how long he was planning to stay in town. He'd told her he'd be leaving on Wednesday.

So he'd be here for three more days.

In the meantime all she could do was carry on as best she could…and pray that Daniel wouldn't stumble on her secret.

"This is your house?" Amy asked, peering out of the car's side window as Willow drew up in the narrow driveway. "It's really pretty, like a storybook picture."

"Yes, it's a sweet little house," Willow said. "But it's not actually ours. It belongs to a couple who used to live here when they were bringing up their children, but now they live in California and they rent the house out to us."

Mikey was bouncing up and down in his car seat. "Out, Willow, out!"

Lizzie had had her nose stuck in a book during the trip from Summerhill but now she looked out, too.

"There's my mom," Willow said, as Gemma appeared at the front door. "She's looking forward to meeting you all."

"I thought your little boy was going to be here," Lizzie said in a tone that gave nothing away.

"Oh, he'll be here," Willow said. "Probably hiding, he's a little bit shy of meeting new people."

She ushered her charges from the car as her mother, all smiles and neatly attired in a white-and-turquoise blouse and white pants, walked down the driveway to meet them.

After all the introductions were made, Gemma said, "Let's go around the back, Willow. Jamie's there."

They followed the path that ran along the side of the house, and entered the backyard, the bottom part of which had been transformed into a play area, with a swing set, teeter-totter, paddling pool, sandbox and a trampoline that Willow had inherited from friends who had moved abroad.

Amy's eyes grew round. "Ooh," she gasped. "Look at that! Can we go play, Willow?"

"Sure. Go ahead."

"Me, too!" Mikey's sturdy legs carried him fast after his sister.

Lizzie hung back, looking around the garden—searching, Willow guessed, for Jamie.

She herself knew where he would be hiding: in his favorite spot on the corrugated iron roof of the toolshed adjacent to the house.

She darted a quick look there and was just in time to see a flash of red before it disappeared. His baseball cap.

Glancing at Lizzie, she saw she was looking in the same direction. She, too, must have seen the flash of red. Ah, well, he'd come down in his own good time.

"Mom," she said, taking her mother's arm, "let's go down to the bottom of the garden, I want to keep a close eye on the little ones. Coming, Lizzie?"

"No," Lizzie said, in an airy nonchalant way that didn't fool Willow. "I want to finish my chapter."

Willow hid a smile. She and her mother exchanged glances as Lizzie walked over to the picnic table by the toolshed. Gemma gave an almost imperceptible nod, and Willow knew she had read her own thoughts.

So she and her mom sauntered off down the close-cropped lawn, leaving Lizzie to approach Jamie in her own way and possibly try to coax him down from his hiding place.

"I still don't know," Willow murmured to her mother, "why Lizzie wants to meet Jamie."

"Mightn't she just want to say she was sorry for having spilled his tray in Morganti's?"

"But why take such a long time to come around to it? Surely if she'd been ashamed of herself and wanted to apologize, she'd have brought the subject up ages ago?"

"Mmm, I agree. Then it must be something else. You've no idea what it could be?"

"No, Mom," she said. "I really don't have a clue."

After a while, she peeked around and saw that instead of Lizzie having coaxed Jamie down from his hiding place, her son had apparently invited Lizzie to come up. The little girl was scrambling over the roof and as Willow watched, she sat down with Jamie and started talking to him.

"Look at that, Mom," she murmured. "I wonder what on earth Lizzie's saying?"

Willow found out, eventually...but not until after she'd driven her charges back to Summerhill that evening and then returned home again.

When she walked into the kitchen she found her mother alone, giving the counters one last swipe with a damp red-and-white checked cloth.

"Where's Jamie?" Willow asked.

"He's in bed—he's bushed. He almost fell asleep in his bath—"

"Mom!" Jamie's voice drifted through from his bedroom. "Is that you?"

"He's waiting for you to read him a story," Gemma said.

"Coming, Jamie," Willow called. "So Mom, what did you think of the Galbraith children?"

"Adorable," Gemma said. "Beautiful children, and very well-mannered. I liked them. Especially Lizzie—although she was very quiet, wasn't she? Is she always so reserved?"

Willow laughed wryly. "Reserved? I'd hardly say so, Mom. She's never pulled any punches when it came to letting me know she resents me. But you're right, she was very quiet today. Unusually so."

"Are you going to ask Jamie what they were talking about?"

"Mmm, when I find the right moment."

Jamie was sitting propped up in bed against his pillows, his book open on his lap. His hair was neatly brushed, his face glowing pink after his bath. As always when she saw him, Willow felt her heart overflow with love.

"Hi, sweetie." She sat on the edge of the bed and when she gave him a bear hug, she noticed that his blue-and-white striped pyjamas still smelled of the sunny summer outdoors after hanging on the line in the backyard.

"Grandma's reached the second last page," he said and yawned. "Can we finish the story tonight?"

"Sure."

Willow started reading, and by the time she reached the end, Jamie's eyes were heavy.

"There." She closed the book and set it aside. "Grandma will have to start a new book tomorrow night."

"I want her to read that one to me again," he said, snuggling under his light covers. "I really liked it."

"And did you like the Galbraith children after all?" she asked, tucking him in.

"Mmm," he said. "We had a lot of fun…"

"Did Lizzie say she was sorry for spilling your tray?"

Jamie's eyelids closed and he said, very drowsily, "Yeah, she did…and she said she'd have told me before if she'd known…"

"Known what, sweetie?"

"If she'd known I didn't ever have a dad. She said she didn't have a mom now, but at least she'd had hers for six years, but I never did have a dad and she thought that was the saddest thing she'd ever heard…but she thought I was doing really well for being a kid without a dad and I should keep it up…and she said she'd be looking for me at school and we'd be friends even if she's older…"

His voice trailed away and seconds later, he was sound asleep.

Willow felt her eyes mist and she swallowed a lump in her throat as she absorbed what he'd told her.

But as she recalled Lizzie's flight from the dining room the previous day, she remembered it had happened right after she'd told Amy that Jamie's dad had died before he was born. She'd been puzzled at the time by Lizzie's behavior; now she realized Lizzie must have been upset by what she'd heard. What a soft heart the child had. The reason Lizzie felt such empathy for Jamie was that she had firsthand experience of being without one parent. And learning of Jamie's loss had not only moved her, but it had made her feel remorse for her rudeness to him in Morganti's and had made her want to offer him kind words of support.

Support that Jamie had obviously appreciated.

Blinking back a tear, Willow brushed a tender kiss over her son's brow, and then tiptoed from the room.

Someday, she would have to tell Jamie who his father was. But she couldn't tell him yet; she'd have to wait till he was old enough to keep a secret. And old enough that Scott Galbraith wouldn't be able to take him away from her.

She had no doubt that the good doctor and his soon-to-be-wife Camryn would provide a warm and loving family life for her treasured little boy, but she was not about to part with her son...not for anything or anyone in the world.

"Hey, Willow...wait up!"

Willow skidded her bike to a halt as she heard Daniel's voice. Tuesday evening, the children were in bed and she'd been given a couple of hours off. She'd decided to go for a ride...and had just trundled her bike from the garage when the familiar voice had stopped her.

One foot on the ground, the other on the pedal, she glanced around apprehensively as she saw Daniel approach.

"Hi." He stopped by her bike. "Where are you off to?"

"Just for a ride, I need some exercise—all that rain earlier today, we were cooped up for hours. So," she said in a deliberately offhand tone, "you're away back to the big city tomorrow."

"That's right."

"Safe trip, then. It was nice of you to come back and visit Mrs. Caird. I know she really appreciated it."

"Least I could do for the old lady. She's all right, is Mrs. C. One of the best. How'd you get on with her?"

"I like her a lot. She says what she thinks, you always know where you are with her."

"Yeah, she hasn't changed." Daniel ran a hand through his blond hair, and his silver earrings glinted in the sun. "She never stood for any crap from me or any of her own kids when she was bringing us up…and we respected her. None of us got involved in boozing or drugs, we'd never have wanted to let her down. Besides, we'd never have dared to—she had an uncanny knack for knowing when somebody was lying."

"I'm sure *you* never told her any lies," Willow teased, trying to inject a lighter moment into their conversation.

"Not as a rule. Only time I used to was when old Chad would have me cover for him. After he'd been out with you, he always told his mother he'd been with me…and once in a while she'd call our place to check…and I always covered for my pal. Mrs. C caught me out once and grounded me for a week." He shook his head. "Poor old Chad. Shame what happened to him." His eyes became wary. "I left here soon after but I gather his folks—being buddy-buddy with the powers-that-be—got the real story hushed up?"

Willow tried to keep her breathing steady, her gaze steady. And her voice steady. "I don't know about anything being hushed up, Daniel. It was an accident, wasn't it? I mean," she forced herself to go on, "you were with Chad when it happened. I only know what was in the local paper—the two of you had climbed up to the roof of the Marsden Tower, and in the dark he stumbled over the parapet and…fell."

"You think that's all there was to it? I mean, you really *believe* that?"

Willow heard the incredulity in his tone and she had a hard time keeping up her show of calm. "Are you telling me that's *not* how it happened?"

"Sheesh, Willow, you and Chad were like that!" He whipped up his right hand, the middle finger crossed tightly over the index finger. "You knew him better'n anybody else at that point in his life—and you couldn't have *not* been aware that the guy was as sure on his feet as a mountain goat! Are you trying to tell me you believe he…he just *stumbled,* and fell to his death…and it was an *accident?*"

"Well, what are *you* trying to say." Willow struggled against a feeling of desperation. "That it *wasn't* an accident?"

The air between them sizzled. Willow was sure he must feel it, too. Her nerves screamed as she waited for his response.

"I always thought you of all people would have figured out what happened that night." His voice was so low she could scarcely hear it. "You must have known that he—"

"Daniel!" Mrs. Caird's voice came floating to them from her apartment window. "Phone call."

"Coming, Ma," he shouted back, without taking his gaze from Willow. "Look, Willow, it's water under the bridge now, but I'm glad I've had this chance to talk to you. It never sat well with me, that Chad died that way, and what made it worse was I could never talk about it with anybody. I wish I could have stopped him, but the state he was in…well, I doubt anybody could have stopped him. Mind you," he said, with a sigh, "I can understand why the family hushed up the truth…they wouldn't have wanted the world to know that he didn't stumble and fall, that he actually *jumped* off that tower—"

Willow choked back an anguished sob.

She hadn't realized, till that very moment, that in her very heart of hearts she had hoped she'd been wrong. She hadn't realized that somewhere, way deep, deep down, she had hoped that Chad's death really had been an accident; that he had really stumbled and fallen, the way the papers had said.

Now, faced with the harsh reality of his suicide, and knowing she had been responsible, she couldn't bear it.

Whirling blindly away from Daniel, she pushed herself up onto her bike again, and ignoring his urgent "Wait, Willow!" She pedaled off down the driveway, hardly able to see where she was going, but knowing only that she had to get away, without a single moment's delay, so that she was alone with her grief when she broke down and wept.

From his study window, Scott watched with a troubled frown as Willow jumped on her bike and took off down the driveway.

He'd been standing there, his mind focused on an article he was studying in a medical journal, when he'd heard a shout outside. And on glancing up casually, he'd seen the nanny skid her bike to a halt and turn to talk with the person who had hailed her.

Daniel Firth. Mrs. Caird's foster son.

Ms. Tyler had told him she barely knew the guy…yet their ensuing conversation had seemed *far* too intense for mere acquaintances.

She had been facing the house as they spoke, and he had had a clear view of her face; and in the moment before she sped away, he had seen that her expression had become distraught. She'd looked as if she was fighting tears.

Dammit, what had that young whipper-snapper said to upset her?

He paced the study, the article forgotten as he wondered what was going on.

And he made up his mind that he wasn't going to bed till she came home and he could ask her what had upset her.

Two hours had elapsed before he caught sight of her trundling her way, wearily, up the hill from the main road.

He knew she would come in through the back door so he quickly made his way there, and by the time she came in, he had a pan of milk simmering on the stove.

"Oh, hi," he said, casually, without looking up. "I thought you'd be back around now—I'm making us some hot chocolate. Take a seat, I'll be right with you."

"Thanks, but I want to go straight to bed—"

"Nonsense. Can't waste this milk!" He arranged his lips in a smile and finally glanced up. And had to exert all his self-control to stifle an angry oath that tried to hiss out when he saw her blotchy face, her swollen red eyelids. Pretending to have noticed nothing out of the ordinary, he said again, "Take a seat." And seeing her hesitate, he said, coaxingly, "I'd like a bit of company."

Her lower lip trembled, and he saw a tear pearl in the corner of one eye. She nodded. But didn't speak. He wondered if she was afraid she might not get any words out.

"The kids have been good," he said, with an assumed cheeriness. "Not a cheep out of any of them…" He chatted on, while he made the hot chocolate, set one mug on the table in front of her, the other on the table across from her and took the chair there. "So," he said, hoping she'd had time to relax a little, "did you enjoy your bike ride?"

She cupped her hands around the mug, then obviously finding it too hot, took her hands away and set them on her lap. He could tell by the play of muscles in her forearm that she was fidgeting, nervously. "Yes." She cleared her throat and gave a tight smile. "Yes, it's a lovely evening. Nice and fresh, after the rain."

"The nights are beginning to close in already," he murmured. "Before we know it, summer will be over. The winters here are pretty harsh, as I recall. Lots of snow. I'm looking forward to taking the kids on the slopes. Do you ski?"

She shook her head.

He gave a light chuckle. "Well, that's four of you I'll have to teach—because you'll have to take the kids to the slopes when I'm on call. Of course, maybe I'm taking too much for granted...I didn't even ask if you'd be interested in taking up the sport. Maybe you're not a cold weather person...?"

"I've always wanted to learn...but it's an expensive hobby. And I've had other...priorities."

"What did you plan to do with your life—before you got pregnant?"

"From the time I was a little girl, I'd wanted to be a teacher. Santa gave me a blackboard when I was seven and from then on, I used to line up my dolls and play school every chance I got. Teaching was my dream."

Her eyes had taken on a faraway look, and he thought how sad it was that she hadn't been able to fulfil her dream. He himself, from the time he was ten, had wanted to be a doctor. He wondered now how he would have coped had that goal been denied him. "You're still young," he said. "One day, maybe…"

"No, it's too late. Heavens, before I know it, it'll be time for Jamie to go to college! Anyway, I'm very happy with what I'm doing now, I'm still working with children, and that's what's important to me."

Their hot chocolate had cooled a little, and he saw her gulp down a mouthful. And then another. He realized that in a moment she'd be getting up from her chair and excusing herself. If he was going to ask her his questions about Firth, he'd better make his move now before she escaped.

"So," he said, tilting back his chair casually, "I saw young Firth out there a while back. You were having a chat with him…"

Her fingers tightened around her mug. She lowered her gaze. "Yes. He's leaving tomorrow."

"You said you didn't know him very well…in the past."

"That's right."

"I just wondered…" He leaned forward and the chair legs snapped to the floor again with a crack like the sound of a whip. "You don't really know him that well…yet you seemed upset this evening, after you talked with him—just as you were after you talked to him on the day he arrived."

He saw her eyes widen, and he knew he'd shocked her. She hadn't, of course, been aware that he'd been privy to those tense interchanges.

"Look," he said, "if something's wrong, I want to help. If Firth has been harassing you, or threatening you in any way, I'll put a stop to it. *Something's* going on between the two of you, Ms. Tyler, but I can't deal with the problem until I know what that problem is. Will you please tell me what Daniel Firth said to you that was so traumatic—''

''It wasn't traumatic!''

''Then why,'' he asked with a weariness that was surpassed only by his impatience, ''have you been crying your eyes out ever since you spoke with him!''

CHAPTER NINE

WILLOW'S initial rush of dismay was drowned out by a feeling of panic.

She had to convince this man, somehow, that nothing was wrong. And yet how could she? He was looking at her now in that intensely penetrating way he had, his blue eyes boring into her with such force she was sure he must know every single thought spinning around in her head.

"Ms. Tyler?" His urging was gentle but determined.

She gripped her hands together in her lap, and though her stomach was churning and her pulse tumbling madly, she made every effort to present a composed exterior.

"Thank you," she said, "for your concern, but I'm all right. What Daniel and I were talking about…it was from the past. He mentioned something I hadn't thought about in years…and you know how it is with memories, they can take you by surprise, throw you off balance, as all the forgotten emotions well up to the surface and…" With a rueful smile, she allowed her words to trail away.

His gaze had hardened. *I am not convinced.*

He didn't utter the words, but he didn't need to; they were written all over his face. She tensed, her throat dry, as she waited for him to press her further.

Glowering at her, he planted his fists squarely on the table. "And you don't want to talk about it?"

"Talking about it won't change anything." And

131

wasn't that an untruth! Talking with him about Chad's death would change everything. Even *thinking* about it, about her part in it, threatened to spill tears from her eyes. She realized she'd better take off before she broke down again.

Abruptly she stood. "If you'll excuse me, I'd like to go up to my room. It's getting late."

Frustration had darkened his eyes, but politeness brought him to his feet. She sensed he was still bursting with questions, so before he could start in on her again, she said, "Good night, Dr. Galbraith," and without waiting for a response, she hastened from the room.

He didn't follow her, didn't even call after her.

And for that, she was truly thankful, because before she got to the stairs she could barely see for her tears.

"Don't forget, Dad, you have to take us to school this afternoon." Amy addressed her father across the breakfast table the next morning as she slipped onto her seat. "For enrollment...and what's the other thing, Lizzie?"

"Orientation." Lizzie pronounced the word with great care. Settling herself in her chair, she added, "Dad, will you take your nose out of your newspaper and listen?"

"Willow says it's rude to read at the table." Amy reached for the cereal packet. "She never allows Lizzie to bring her book to the dining room."

Willow strapped Mikey into his chair and avoided looking at her employer as he snapped the newspaper aside. She'd been hoping he'd already gone to the clinic. No such luck.

"So," he drawled, "Ms. Tyler has been telling you I'm guilty of bad manners."

Startled, Willow flicked her head up and said, "No, of course not. I didn't—"

"You didn't use me as an example?" His eyes had an amused gleam. "An example of how *not* to behave at the table?"

"I'm concerned with the *children's* manners." She poured Mikey's cereal, and added milk. "But it's certainly not my place to criticize yours." Taking her own seat, she helped herself to toast and butter. "And I never have."

"It's okay, Dad," Amy reassured him. "Willow never says bad things about you. Just good stuff."

"Ah." The corners of his mouth twitched. "What kind of good stuff?"

Amy wrinkled her nose as she cast her mind back. "We…ell, at her house on Sunday, I was hiding behind a bush, being real quiet when we were playing hide-and-seek with Jamie, and Willow walked by with her mom and I heard her say you were prob'ly the nicest man she'd ever met."

Willow blushed wildly. What else had she said? Even as she racked her brains trying to remember, she said in a rush, "Amy, do eat up, your cereal's going to get soggy!"

Amy waved her spoon, dismissing Willow vaguely as she continued, "And not only that, she said you were drop-dead gorgeous and she was having an awful job trying to stop herself from falling in love with you." She finally came to a stop, and beamed at her father. "That's all good stuff, Dad…isn't it?"

Willow prayed for a miracle; for an earthquake that would crack the floor open right under her feet—

A choking sound came from across the table and she saw that Amy's father looked as if he were about to have an apoplectic fit. The sounds coming from his mouth could have meant anything…Willow wasn't sure if he was trying not to laugh…or trying not to cry.

Whatever, it didn't bode well for her. Or for her continued tenure at Summerhill. Even as she felt nervous perspiration prickle her upper lip, and she braced herself to hear whatever he had to say next, the door opened and Mrs. Caird came in.

"Dr. Galbraith, I've just had a phone call from my daughter Angie's husband. Angie's in labor, she seems to be having problems, he's taking her to the hospital now and he wants you to come. Right away."

It wasn't an earthquake, but the effect was as good as.

Muttering "Excuse me," the doctor pushed himself to his feet, and without letting his eyes so much as flick in Willow's direction, he followed Mrs. Caird from the room. Seconds later, Willow heard the front door slam shut. Then another minute later, she heard his car roar away down the driveway.

She slumped back in her seat, as limp as if she'd been churned through a wringer. What a disaster…

Lizzie was old enough to know it, and was tittering.

Mikey was shoveling cereal into his mouth, oblivious to the little melodrama that had gone on around him.

Amy was looking eagerly at her nanny, her guileless blue eyes wide, her expression seeking approval.

Willow gave the child a helpless smile. Oh, Amy, she thought in despair. What *have* you done! In trying to defend me, you've put me in an impossible situation. And put your father in a worse one.

How on earth was she going to face him now?

And how long would it be before he came back from

the hospital and said to her the words she was dreading:
Pack your bags, Ms. Tyler. You're fired!

"Thank you so much, Dr. Galbraith." Angie Pratt
brushed back a lock of damp hair that had fallen over
her brow. "I don't know how I'd have managed without
you!"

Scott looked down at the new mom and her first baby,
nicely settled in the maternity ward after a long and very
difficult birth. "You're the one who did all the work,
Angie—and I'm sure you think it was worth it, now
that it's all over."

"They say women forget about the pain as soon as
the baby's born—and they don't remember it until they
go into labor the next time around...and by then it's
too late!"

Scott laughed. "Yeah, I've heard that before. Well,
I'll have to be on my way. I'm taking my own kids to
the school this afternoon, have to enroll them."

Angie's husband, Tom, rounded the bed and shook
the doctor's hand. "Thanks again, you were great. I
have to admit that when we heard Dr. McRae was re-
tiring, we were worried, she'd been our family doctor
for years. But you're great, top-notch, one terrific doctor."

As Scott drove home, he found Tom Pratt's words
echoing in his head...and he blew out a heavy sigh.
This, it seemed, was his day for receiving compliments.
Not only was he apparently one terrific doctor, he reflected ironically, but he was also "drop-dead gorgeous."

He hadn't had time since leaving Summerhill that
morning, to think about Amy's remarks at the breakfast
table. Now they returned with the force of a slap.

Good grief, he'd almost choked when he'd heard her repeat what Ms. Tyler had said to her mother. His fears had been realized. The nanny did fancy him. Was actually on the verge of falling in love with him.

And dammit, he didn't want that to happen.

She was an excellent nanny and he didn't want to lose her. Didn't want to fire her.

He and Ms. Tyler were going to have to talk.

But they wouldn't have time to discuss the matter now; they had to be at the school by three. It was already twenty to the hour. This evening, then, after the children were in bed. He'd discuss the matter with her then...and he'd just have to hope the right words would come out.

The words that would kill her budding attraction to him.

When he pulled the car up in the forecourt, he saw her come out the front door. Alone. Pausing on the top step, she raised a hand to her brow to shade her eyes from the sun. And then, she walked down the steps to meet him.

He got out and slammed the car door.

"Where are the children?" he asked. "Are they ready?"

"Well, no...they're still in their rooms."

"Don't we have to be at the school at three?"

"No, three-thirty."

"Oh. I thought it was three." So...what did she want with him? Why had she come to meet him?

"I wanted to talk to you where Mrs. Caird wouldn't overhear." Her face seemed very pale. "About...what Amy said to you this morning."

He had to admire her for her courage. This couldn't have been an easy step for her—

"I know you can't want me around anymore, but…" Her eyes were anguished but she went on bravely. "It's the children, you see. Mikey, and Amy, and Lizzie. We've formed a…bond—oh, I can't claim to have won Lizzie over yet, but I'm making headway, slowly… and…" She took in a deep breath and went on in a rush, "I think it would do great harm if I were to disappear from their lives now. Another rug being pulled from under their feet. I honestly don't think they could cope with it…Lizzie especially. She's so vulnerable, they all are." She twisted her hands together, the movement as anguished as her expression. "So won't you please try to forget what happened this morning? Not for my sake, of course, but for—"

"Ms. Tyler." She was going to start weeping. And he couldn't stand it. She talked about Lizzie being vulnerable? For pity's sake, she herself was more vulnerable than any female he'd ever met. And he had to prevent her from weeping because if he saw tears spilling from her eyes he wouldn't be able to stop himself from reaching out to her, taking her in his arms, comforting her…and that would be disastrous. What he had to do was distance himself from her. And distance her from him. He knew there was only one way to do it. Make her angry.

"Yes?" She quavered.

"You're making far too much of what happened this morning. Did you think I was surprised by what Amy said? Did you think I was *shocked* to hear you were falling in love with me?" He gave an amused laugh. "Actually my only surprise has been that it didn't happen sooner, since I'm far from being an unattractive man—"

She gave a little gasp. He barged on ruthlessly.

"I do see myself daily in the mirror when I shave, Ms. Tyler. I know that I'm what writers of romantic novels describe as 'tall, dark and handsome,' a combination the opposite sex apparently find irresistible. I'm also a widower, which appeals to the female's mothering instinct. And lastly, but certainly not leastly!—I'm a doctor. Women find it *amazingly* easy to fall in love with doctors…maybe it's because we seem like gods to them, or maybe it's because of our bedside manners—"

"Dr. Galbraith." She had drawn her petite figure to its full height and outrage sizzled from her every pore. "You have the bedside manners of a skunk and you have the tact of a…a rhinoceros and you have the conceit of a…a peacock!" She tossed her head and he couldn't help noticing how beautifully her silky hair glinted in the sun.

Out of nowhere, he was reminded of a long-ago fishing trip in the Scottish Highlands, of silver trout slipping through a brandy-colored stream—no, not a stream, over there they called it a burn—the estate factor had referred to it as "a burrrn."

"You're not even listening!" Ms. Tyler had planted her dainty fists on her dainty hips. "Well, listen to this, Dr. Tall Dark and Handsome. I'm staying here. I'm not going to desert your children. And if you try to fire me, I'll take the case all the way to the Supreme Court if necessary. So I was in danger of falling in love with you." She curled her upper lip as if she were smelling something unpleasant. "But you may rest assured that after this little conversation, that danger is now well and truly over!"

She spun around and stalked regally back to the steps, while he watched, torn between admiration for her guts, and a deep heartfelt regret that he'd had to give this sweet young woman such a false impression of the man he really was.

But it had been necessary.

He was going to marry Camryn.

That was his Perfect Plan.

And he was going to let nothing get in its way.

Especially not the insistent but totally inappropriate drag of attraction he felt for his plain-Jane nanny!

From that day on, though Willow's attitude to her three charges remained the same as it had always been, her attitude toward their father changed. She was always polite and cooperative, but she was withdrawn. Distant. Her tone was flat when she talked to him; her gaze was flat when she looked at him.

If he noticed—and how could he not?—he made no comment. His attitude had changed, too. He had taken to treating her in a way she could describe only as "vigorous." His smiles were wide but impersonal; his manner brisk; his conversation—on the occasions when communication was necessary—was blunt.

He addressed her in the way she'd heard sailors address each other in old pirate movies: bluff and hale and sturdy. She wouldn't have been in the least surprised if he'd started sprinkling his speech with salty "me hearties!" or started calling "Avast there!" after her when he needed her, instead of his customary "Hang on a minute!"

The atmosphere between them was highly charged and by the time Friday rolled around—the day of the Moffats's party—Willow had a constant tension headache.

She hated discord of any kind, and though she and

her employer weren't openly fighting, the under-the-surface conflict was even more upsetting than outright hostilities.

She dreaded the evening ahead.

She dreaded having to present a happy front to the Moffats, dreaded being in the same room with Scott Galbraith for what would be hours on end. The very last thing she felt like doing was going to a social function!

The children, of course, were looking forward to it immensely and their bedrooms were filled with noise and squeals of excitement as Willow supervised their dressing.

Once the trio were ready, she lined them up in the girls' room, like soldiers.

"Inspection time," she said, smiling. "And I have to say—" she straightened Mikey's bow tie "—you all pass muster."

"But I don't *like* mustard," Amy fretted.

"That's not what it means," Lizzie said.

"What *does* it mean?" Amy asked anxiously.

"It means," Lizzie said, "that we're okay."

"Oh. Well, goody!" Amy twirled around so fast she lost balance and bumped into Mikey who fell sideways against Lizzie and jolted her so she tumbled back onto her bed.

Willow could see a fight in the offing. Before it could get going, she said quickly, "Oh, my goodness, will you look at that!"

"What?" they chorused.

Willow crossed to the window. "It's raining." She hadn't noticed that the day had darkened, but now she could see that black clouds covered the sky, and heavy rain was sweeping the countryside.

"We'll need to wear coats," Amy said, wrinkling her nose. "We don't want to get our new dresses wet!"

"Dad's home." Lizzie pressed a fingertip to the window-pane, pointing down to the forecourt where her father's car was drawing in. "He'll have to hurry up and get dressed or we're going to be late." She swiveled her gaze to Willow and ran a frowning glance over Willow's T-shirt and jeans. "You'd better hurry too. You can't go in *that* old outfit."

"She's not." Amy looked up. "You're going to wear the dress you bought at Aunt Camryn's, *aren't* you, Willow?"

"I'm going to change now. While I'm doing that, will you get out your rain slickers and rubber boots? We'll pack your shoes in a bag and take them with us."

"We'll put on our raincoats now," Lizzie said. "And then Dad won't see our dresses till we get to the party. That way, he'll get an even bigger and better surprise!"

"Oh, goody!" Amy jumped up and down. "And you, too, Willow. You put your coat on and when we get to the party we'll all whisk them off together and Dad will get such a surprise he'll be—" She gnawed her lip. "He'll be what, Lizzie? What's the word that he'll be?"

"He'll be stunned." Lizzie loved being asked for help when it came to finding the right word. "He's going to be absolutely stunned."

The day at the clinic had been even busier than usual.

Scott had seen eight patients by lunchtime, and in the early afternoon he'd had to hurry to the hospital to perform an emergency C-section. When he returned to the clinic, his appointments had backed up, and it was twenty to five before he'd seen the last patient.

When he left the clinic, the day had become dark. It was starting to rain, and by the time he got home it was coming down heavily. As he dashed from the car to the front door, the rain sluiced over him.

Once inside, he stood for a moment, catching his breath, shaking off raindrops. From upstairs, he could hear giggles and the sound of light footsteps as his children scampered around. They'd be up to high doh, of course, anxious to get to the party. He himself would have given anything to be able to stay home, with his feet up, a glass of beer in his hand—

"Get changed, Dad!" Amy's disembodied voice drifted down to him. "We're all ready—but you can't see us because we want to give you a surprise!" Doors slammed. The house became quiet.

Where, he wondered, was Ms. Tyler?

Not that he was keen to see her, he reflected as he ascended the stairs. Since Tuesday, anytime they'd been in the same room the tension in the air had been so thick he'd wanted to punch a hole in it. He hated the feeling of discord between them. Actually he hated discord of any kind.

He reached the landing and heard muffled sounds from behind bedroom doors. Still no sign of Ms. Tyler.

Which was good. Wasn't it? He needed to relax and there was no relaxing when that woman was around!

He went into his own room, and shut the door firmly.

After a quick shower, he opened his closet door and was hesitating over which suit to wear, when he noticed a navy blazer tucked at the end of the rack, at the back.

The blazer had been there since his last visit to Summerhill…but he'd been so distraught when he left to go home that he'd somehow omitted to pack it. He'd taken off right after Chad's funeral…taken off quickly, as had the rest of the family, unable to bear another moment in this place, fresh as it was with its painful memories.

He wondered, now, if the jacket would still fit him. He'd spent a lot of time at the gym in the months after Chad's death—had driven himself mercilessly, in the same way as he'd driven himself relentlessly at work in an attempt to obliterate his grief...and the feelings of guilt that he hadn't been there for Chad when—

With an effort, he tore his thoughts from the unhappy past and concentrated on the present.

He slipped the blazer on, and when he found it still fit perfectly, he decided to wear it. Chad was dead; he had come to grips with that some time ago. What mattered was today. *Only* today.

And today held its own problems. Problems that were all tied up with Ms. Tyler—who had fancied herself in love with him but now despised him.

The Moffats would surely notice the tension between them and he didn't want to mar their evening by bringing discord into their home. He'd have to talk privately with Ms. Tyler and ask her—order her, if necessary!—to put her contempt for him on the back burner.

A few minutes later he left his bedroom, sporting the blazer with a pair of gray flannels, a crisp white shirt and a navy-and-silver striped tie.

The children, and Willow, were waiting in the hall. They looked up at him as he ran down the stairs, Amy and Lizzie smiling, Mikey jumping around, Ms. Tyler still and silent, sending out invisible waves of dislike.

His offspring were wearing yellow rain slickers and red rubber boots; she was in a shiny black cape and black rubber boots. Like the children, she had pulled the hood of her cape over her head, and the darkness

of the cape was reflected in her eyes. Eyes that were
regarding him now with a gaze that cut him, and made
him want to swear.

Instead he addressed the children. "All set?"

"Yes, Dad!"

"Right, then." He took his golfing umbrella from the
hall closet and opened the front door. A gust of wind
blew a spatter of rain into the entryway. "Give me a
sec to open all the car doors and then the rest of you
make a run for it. Lizzie, I want you to sit in the front
with me—Ms. Tyler can sit in back and keep Mikey
and Amy amused."

By the time her employer drew his car up in front of
the Moffats's grand Tudor house, Willow felt sick with
nerves. When he had come downstairs earlier, she'd noticed how strained he looked. He'd had an exhausting
day, that was obvious. And no matter that she knew she
ought to despise him for his arrogance and conceit, she
still found herself worrying about him. A man as busy
as he was at work needed peace and quiet in his leisure
hours. He'd expected her to keep Amy and Mikey
amused on the drive and she'd made a poor job of it.
They were high with excitement and she couldn't get
them to settle. They'd squabbled all the way, and it
wasn't till they left the main road and turned onto the
Moffats's driveway that they finally gave up on their
bickering.

Their father hadn't said a word, but his shoulders had
become rigid, and Willow had seen his knuckles whiten
as he tightened his grip on the steering wheel.

When he switched off the engine, she wasted no time
in opening the car door and ushering the two little ones
out onto the driveway.

The rain had stopped about fifteen minutes earlier, and the air smelled pleasantly of damp earth and roses. Lizzie had shoved her door open and as she got out, she grabbed Mikey's hand and took off.

"Where are you going?" Amy shouted.

"Around the back!"

"Wait for me!" Amy scurried after them.

Willow made to follow, but her employer slammed his door and walked around the car, saying "Hang on a minute."

His voice, for the first time in days, didn't have that "Avast, me hearties!" tone. It was low, and serious.

Taking in an apprehensive breath, Willow turned to face him. He was going to let her have it, she guessed, for being unable to control Amy and her brother. Now, even as she steeled herself for his reprimand, she was hopelessly aware of how attractive he was in his navy blazer and flannels. Just looking at him made her knees weak.

"We have to talk." He came to a halt in front of her. "Before we go inside."

"I know." She sighed. "I'm sorry, I should have been able to keep them quiet, and I could see how uptight you were getting with all their squabbling—"

"Yes, I'm uptight…but not about that. It's this— whatever's going on between the two of *us* that's bothering me. A party should be a happy occasion. Can we agree—for the sake of the Moffats and the rest of their guests—to put all our differences aside, just for the next few hours? Then—" his eyes took on a sardonic, mocking gleam "—you can go back to despising me openly, as you have been doing for the past several days."

CHAPTER TEN

"A TRUCE?" Willow was surprised—and relieved—that this was what he'd wanted to discuss. "I don't have any problem with that. And pretending not to despise you shouldn't be too hard," she added, dryly. "I studied drama in high school and always got straight *A*'s for acting."

She saw his lips twitch, but before he could reply, Camryn came out the front door, looking elegant in a black dress with bold silver accessories.

She greeted Scott with a peck on the cheek.

"Where are the children?" she asked.

He said, "They've gone around to the back door."

"Good. Mom's in the kitchen with Cook, she'll give them a snack to hold them till dinner." Camryn turned to Willow. "It's lovely to see you again, Willow. Come away inside, I'll take you upstairs and you can take off your cape."

She looped her arm through Scott's as they all walked to the front door. "What a blessing the rain has stopped. Wasn't it ghastly there for a while? I imagine the drive here was pretty hairy. Anyway," she went on as she ushered them into the house, "you're the first to arrive so you'll have a chance to relax before the other guests start turning up—we don't expect them till closer to seven."

She closed the front door behind them and Willow had scarcely time to take in the enormous foyer with its Persian carpets and dark furniture and sparkling chandelier, before Camryn was escorting her up the staircase while calling back to Scott, ''Dad's in the lounge, he'll pour you a drink.''

Camryn chatted away to Willow as she led her along a corridor, and into what was obviously a guest room. Decorated in peach and sage-green, with a bow window looking out over rolling hills, it smelled of lavender and was one of the prettiest rooms Willow had ever seen. She was admiring it when Camryn murmured a soft ''Tsk!''

''I forgot I had this window open,'' she said. ''The rain has come in, it's all over the sill. Excuse me for a moment, Willow, while I get a cloth to wipe it up. Take your cape off, you'll find hangers in the closet.''

After Willow had disposed of her cape, she scrutinized her reflection in the closet's mirrored door.

She had debated earlier whether to pull her hair back into a ponytail, or leave it loose. In the end, she'd decided to leave it loose. But somehow, she didn't look right and she wasn't sure why. Oh, the dress was lovely—though it had looked *nothing* on the hanger at the boutique, just a slither of shapeless silk. But when she'd put it on, she'd been amazed at how the fabric had clung in just the right places, and how the glorious shade of sea-green had suited her, making her eyes glow.

''That dress could have been made for you, Willow!'' Camryn swept across the room, waving a rag toward Willow. ''But your hair should be up. I'll style it for you, if you don't mind, once I've mopped up this mess.'' She busied herself at the window. ''You don't mind, do you, dear?''

''No of course not, but it's not necessary, really.''

Camryn turned to Willow and said with a teasing

twinkle in her eye, "Oh, but it is. You're wearing a Camryn Moffat dress so you're a walking advertisement for my designs and I won't settle for anything less than perfection."

Scott felt frustrated beyond belief.

And it was all because of his children's nanny.

Not that he could fault her attitude toward him; she'd behaved impeccably all evening, particularly during the buffet-style dinner where by chance they'd ended up sitting together. Now they were in the lounge, where everyone had drifted after their coffee, and while guests fussed over the children, she'd remained discreetly in the background, obviously attempting to blend into the woodwork as any good nanny would.

The problem was…she wasn't blendable.

Not in that slinky sea-green dress, not with her hair swept up in that sexy little top-knot, not with her long legs so tantalizingly set off by those strappy high-heeled sandals.

And just look at her now, he reflected morosely as he stood alone, nursing a drink. Look at her smiling as she's chatted up by Lex Brennen, the Moffats's twenty-something bachelor neighbor, just back from a success-ful Everest climb. Tanned within an inch of his life and a dead ringer for Pierce Brosnan, the guy oozed cha-risma and had knocked every woman in the room for six—

"Scott…"

He dragged his gaze away from the couple as Camryn appeared at his side. "Oh, hi, there…"

"Oops, why the surly growl? Are you annoyed with me for inviting the children to sleep over? After Willow and I put them to bed, it did occur to me that it was a bit presumptuous of me to whisk them off the way I did, but they were so tired and I was afraid that if you noticed they were getting cranky you'd pack them into the car and take them home, and I didn't want you to cut your evening short—''

"No, it's okay that they're staying over." Oh, sure. It was okay that he was now stuck with driving the nanny home, alone; it was okay that he was now stuck with spending the night at Summerhill with her, alone. It was okay that every time he looked at her, he wanted to drag her into his arms and kiss her till her head spun? "I appreciate the thought and I certainly wouldn't want to break up the party. I'll drive over tomorrow morning and pick them up."

"Why don't we wait and see how things go? They start school next week, it would be nice for us to have them for the weekend. I'll call you tomorrow, let you know. Meanwhile," she added, "would you do me a favor?"

"Yeah?"

"I'm going to ask everybody to stand to one side for a bit and could you get hold of…let me see…Lex…and ask him to roll back the carpet? Then could you take Willow through to the den and show her where the stereo is? I've had more speakers put in since last you were here—the music gets piped through to the lounge now."

"Why do you want Willow to know where the stereo is?"

"I've delegated her to go through our collection and choose the music—did you know she's won *umpteen* medals for dancing?" Camryn walked away, saying over her shoulder, "Apparently she's studied jazz and ballet since she was old enough to walk!"

He hoped that Willow would stay in the den for the rest of the evening, so he wouldn't have to look at her!

Putting down his glass on the nearest surface, he tried his best not to scowl as he threaded his way across the room to where she was still standing with the Everest hero.

"Excuse me," he said. "Sorry to break this up, Brosnan—"

"Name's Brennen." The man interrupted mildly. "Three *n*'s, two *e*'s."

Scott could have kicked himself for the slip. And could have kicked the man for his movie star good looks and for standing so close to the nanny that their arms touched. "Brennen. Sorry. Camryn wants you to roll back the carpet for dancing."

"Dancing? Terrific!" Brennen flashed Willow a smile that was all white teeth and mahogany tan and bedroom eyes. "Sweetie, we'll have a dance later so save me a place on your card!"

He strode off, whistling, and Scott scowled after him.

"You seem annoyed with me," the nanny said somewhat stiffly. "What have I done to upset you?"

Scott swiveled his gaze back to her. And when he saw her troubled expression, he felt a wave of shame. The fact that he desired her, physically, was *his* problem. Taking his frustration out on her was unfair. She'd never in any way set out to attract him. On the contrary.

He said quietly, "You've done nothing to upset me, Willow. Absolutely nothing. You've behaved perfectly, and I want to thank you for hiding the way you feel about me. I appreciate it. Now…Camryn tells me you're going to be choosing the music for dancing, and she's asked me to take you through to the den and show you where the stereo is."

"I hope you don't mind my helping Camryn out—I really wanted to stay upstairs with the children."

"They're sound asleep. What would be the point? And of course I don't mind."

What he *did* mind was the effect her perfume had on him as she walked beside him along the corridor. He hadn't noticed it in the car because she'd been sitting in the back. But now it drifted to him, elusive, subtle, sensual. Essence of Temptation. If that wasn't its name, he decided with a feeling of despair, then it should be.

"Here we are," he announced as he escorted her into the den. "And there's the stereo system."

Her eyes widened. "Oh, my, what an elaborate setup."

"Yeah, I wouldn't mind having one like it installed at Summerhill." He opened a cabinet packed with discs, all neatly arranged, alphabetically labeled.

"Thanks." She crouched by the cabinet, her expression eager. "Oh, some of my favorites…" She pulled out discs, setting them on the carpet. "Wonderful…"

He knew by her tone that she was speaking to herself, and had forgotten he was there. He also knew he should leave her to it, and not give in to his desire to run a hand over her top-knot, feel the silky texture of her hair.

He cleared his throat. "I'll be off then."

Vaguely she murmured, "Mmmm…"

So he left the room, but instead of returning to the lounge, he made his way to the back of the house, and into the kitchen where the cook was taking a load of steaming plates from the dishwasher.

"That was a terrific meal," he said as she gave him a smile, her round face flushed and damp with perspiration. "Once again you outdid yourself, Bettina."

"Thank you, Dr. Galbraith. I'm glad you enjoyed it."

''We all did.'' He rounded the island and crossed to the back door. ''I'm going to take a turn outside,'' he said. ''I need to get away from the crowd for a bit. If anyone comes looking for me, Bettina, you haven't seen me!''

She raised her eyebrows and looked at him blankly. ''Seen who?''

He chuckled, and was still chuckling as he closed the door behind him and strolled out into the starry night.

''I *thought* I'd find you hiding up here!''

When Willow heard Camryn whisper the words to her from the doorway of the darkened bedroom, she got up silently from the chair by Amy's bed and tiptoed across the carpet.

''I'm not really hiding,'' she whispered. ''After I got the music going I popped up here to check on the children and I found Amy awake—she said she was thirsty. I got her a glass of water but she was grumpy and out of sorts, and it took some time for her to fall asleep again, and since she seemed restless I decided I'd better stay awhile.''

''And now?'' Camryn looked over her shoulder. ''As far as I can see, the child's still as a mouse!''

''Yes, she *has* settled now but—''

Camryn took her by the arm and tugged her out into the corridor. ''No buts, Willow.'' Shutting the door firmly, she drew a reluctant Willow along to the landing. ''It's a *lovely* party. You must come down and have some fun.''

''I'm not here to have fun, Camryn. I'm here to look after the children.''

''Which you have done admirably. But all work and no play make Willow a dull girl. And I promise I'll allow you to go upstairs and look in on them every fifteen minutes!''

She was teasing, but she was so nice, and so friendly, Willow decided not to protest further. And she had to admit—if only to herself—that she didn't *really* want to. While up in Amy's room, she'd heard the insistent beat of the stereo, as it drifted faintly upstairs, and she'd found herself tapping her feet. The urge to dance, when she heard music, was as always, an irresistible temptation. So with a wry sigh, she picked up her step...and felt her heartbeats quicken, too, as she and Camryn ran lightly down the stairs.

Lex Brennen was crossing the hall toward the lounge. When he saw them, his face lit up in a charming smile.

''Camryn,'' he said, ''your knight in shining armor has finally turned up, just as your mother was about to send out a search party—apparently he went for a walk, and lost his bearings. But all is well, and the warrior has returned—he was recently spotted out on the patio, communing with the stars.''

Camryn laughed. ''It's like drawing blood from a stone,'' she said, ''to get that man onto a dance floor. Genevieve swore that the only time she'd ever succeeded was at their wedding reception...and then only because it couldn't be avoided.''

A man who didn't like to dance. Willow felt sorry for him. What he was missing!

As they all walked into the lounge, Willow saw that several couples were jiving to the lively music. Camryn's parents were seated around a coffee table with Snead Gallagher, a retired lawyer. The French doors were open, and a dark figure stood outside, alone, at the far end of the patio. Scott. He looked...solitary.

Camryn's mother called out, "Camryn, darling, come here a moment—we need you to settle an argument…"

Camryn excused herself, and Lex said to Willow, "Now, sweetheart—" he grasped her hand in a masterful grip "—we'll have that dance you promised me!"

She certainly wasn't his sweetheart, and she certainly hadn't promised him a dance. But it would be rude to refuse, so Willow let him lead her onto the dance floor.

Her partner, she soon discovered to her surprise and delight, was a *fabulous* dancer. And so—as she always did when she landed so lucky—she gave herself up to the joy of the moment and the rhythm of the music, and within moments had forgotten about everything else.

He was being rude and he knew it.

Scott turned irritably from his mindless scrutiny of the Moffats's garden, with its discreetly lit paths, its illuminated fountain and its pretty white-painted gazebo. He should go inside…the only reason he'd taken off was that he couldn't stand being around Willow.

What was wrong with him? Why was he so obsessed with her? And no, obsessed *wasn't* too strong a word; it was his obsession with her that was ruining his evening.

And it was ridiculous.

If he were any older, he'd think he was having a midlife crisis. Hankering after a child-bride. But he was nowhere near midlife…still, he should be hankering after someone closer to his own age.

He should be hankering after *Camryn*.

What he had to do, he decided grimly, was get a hold of his sister-in-law, take her to some shadowy corner of the garden, haul her into his arms and kiss her. Kiss her

till they were both awash in lust and passion...kiss her
till he ached to make love to her.

And then, at that point where he'd forgotten the
nanny and everything else...he had to propose marriage.

Marriage to Camryn.

It was a Perfect Plan.

And as he opened the French doors and entered the
lounge, he decided to move on it without a second's
delay—

He stopped short just inside the room, his Perfect
Plan momentarily forgotten.

The music was pulsing in the kind of primal beat that
stirred a man to primal lust; stirred him at least! But the
only people dancing were Brennen and the nanny. The
other dancers had moved to the fringes of the floor to
watch—and boy, were the two ever something to watch.

But he himself had eyes only for Willow as she
laughingly teased her partner with her spinning and her
weaving, and with provocative body movements and
steps so fast her long legs were a blur...and all the
while, the beat drummed on, till his head pounded with
it.

And all the while, she was oblivious to him and to
everyone else but the man she was flirting with—her
eyes sparkling, her smile teasing, her sea-green dress
fluttering around her like the silken wings of a tropical
bird.

Scott leaned back against the doorjamb, his mouth
dry, his knees weak.

She was a woman transformed.

Seduction personified.

The music rose to a climax, Brennen snaked out a
hand to catch hers, and in a final triumphant whirl, they

brought the dance to an end as the music ended in a reverberating drumroll.

Silence reigned…and then wild applause broke out. Everyone crowded around the couple, voices raised in praise.

"That was wonderful—"

"Wow, what a stupendous performance!"

"Ms. Tyler—" that was his father-in-law "—I used to think Ginger Rogers could dance, but…"

Everyone's voices joining in the clamor.

Urgings for an encore.

Scott swiveled around and went out again to the patio. Dammit, he thought desperately, what am I to do? Rubbing a distraught hand over his nape, he walked across the patio, and started down the path leading to the gazebo.

He had almost reached the picturesque white structure when he heard a voice coming from behind. "Scott…"

He turned. It was Camryn.

The timing, he realized, couldn't have been better.

He waited for her to catch up with him. And as she stepped lightly toward him, he let his gaze run over her—over her beautiful familiar face; over her mane of glorious black hair; over her tall and voluptuous figure.

"Hey," he said when she reached him, "I'm glad you came out." He took her hand, twined his fingers with hers. "Let's find somewhere we can be alone. I have something to say to you, Camryn, and I don't want us to be disturbed."

Willow saw him take off.

She'd noticed him just before he turned to leave, and the expression on his face had chilled her.

She'd really done it now, she thought despairingly. She'd made an exhibition of herself; had drawn attention to herself, which was an absolute no-no where nannies were concerned. They were supposed to be seen and not heard—and preferably not even seen!

As her employer disappeared out onto the patio, she turned her attention to Lex, who was laughingly saying he was far too exhausted for an encore, he couldn't keep up with his partner. Willow joined in the laughter, but inwardly breathed a sigh of relief. And within minutes she was able to slip quietly away.

She went upstairs to check on the children. She found Lizzie and her brother both asleep; and when she checked on Amy, she found her asleep, too.

She wandered aimlessly over to the bedroom window, which looked down on the gardens. They were deserted—except for a tall dark figure walking toward the gazebo.

Scott.

She knew she had to apologize to him, and now, perhaps, would be a good opportunity while he was alone.

Ignoring the way her heart had leaped at the sight of him, and without giving herself time to mull over her decision, she hurried from the room, ran down the stairs, and wanting to avoid the party, went outside via the kitchen door.

She made her way to the gardens, and walked over the lawn toward the gazebo.

But when she reached it, no one was there.

He must have walked farther on.

Or perhaps he'd already retraced his steps and returned to the house.

A puffy cloud drifted over the moon, putting everything into deep shadow. At the same time, from the trees nearby came the soft hoot of an owl, followed by the increasingly loud roar of a motorcycle, passing by on the main road.

Willow mounted the wooden steps leading up to the gazebo, and sank down on a cushioned seat. Closing her eyes, she leaned back with a sigh, and listened as the harsh sound of the motorcycle gradually faded away, leaving the night once again enveloped in silence.

It was then that she heard a voice. Her employer's voice. So close that her heart almost stopped.

Then, before she could move, she heard another voice.

Camryn's.

Heart thudding, Willow pushed herself to her feet, preparing to make her presence known. She peered into the shadowy night, uncomfortable that she was intruding on a private conversation.

The cloud that had glided over the moon now glided on past it; and in its white beams Willow saw the couple. And when she saw them, dismay sucked the breath from her lungs.

Scott and his sister-in-law were standing a mere ten feet from the gazebo, and he had his arms around her. But even as Willow tried to decide whether she ought to cough to announce her presence or try to sneak away unseen, she heard Scott say, in a voice that held more than a hint of desperation,

"Will you marry me, Camryn?"

Clamping a hand over her mouth to suppress a cry of distress, Willow finally managed to move. Wrenching off her sandals, she clutched them in her hands as she crept silently from the gazebo and fled back into the house.

Thankfully, when she burst breathlessly into the kitchen, there was no one there to see her distress.

And she was fortunate that she met no one as she slipped upstairs. But as she stumbled along the corridor leading to the children's rooms, she noticed that Lizzie's bedroom door was open. And across the way, the bathroom door was ajar, the light was on, and as she hurried to investigate, she heard sounds of retching coming from inside the bathroom.

Hesitantly she pushed the door open.

Lizzie, shivering and sobbing, was kneeling over the toilet, her hands clawed around the toilet seat as she choked and gagged, sick but with nothing left to come up.

"Oh, Lizzie!" Willow quickly kneeled beside her. Stroking her back, she felt it chilled even through the long white T-shirt the child was wearing. "Why didn't you come down and tell me you weren't feeling well."

"It was my own fault." Lizzie sat back on her heels, and wretchedly shoved back her damp, sticky hair from her flushed cheeks. "Cook warned me after dinner not to eat any more chocolate cake but I snuck another two slices. Then when I started to feel sick a little while ago, I...I did go looking for you," she said, gulping back tears. She leaned over the toilet again, gagging, and then fell limply against the edge of the bath.

"I think," she said in a small voice, "that I won't be sick again. I feel it's all up now."

She didn't fight as Willow used a warm damp cloth to wipe her face and brush back her damp hair. All the while, she fixed glassy blue eyes on her nanny, eyes that were so miserable that Willow felt her heart go out to her.

"So you came looking for me," Willow murmured.
"Couldn't you find me?"

"Well, I crept downstairs but when I peeked in the
lounge I saw you dancing with Mr. Brennen and you
were having fun and I didn't want to spoil—"

"Oh, Lizzie." Willow couldn't help herself; at the
risk of being rejected, she tenderly drew the chilled, thin
figure into her arms and held her close. "I don't care
two hoots about dancing with Mr. Brennen. What I care
about is you. You and Mikey and Amy. I'm here to
look after you, that's my job but it's not just a job. It's
what I love doing. I love you all and I *want* to look
after you."

Lizzie slumped bonelessly against her, and hugging
her close, Willow started to hum, and then sing softly,
Brahm's lullaby, which never failed to soothe Jamie if
he was out of sorts.

Willow felt her heart leap with joy as Lizzie's slender
arms crept around her and small fingers clutched the
back of the sea-green dress. With her face buried against
the nanny's bosom, she whispered, "That's the song
Mommy used to sing to me."

"You loved her a lot, didn't you, sweetheart, and you
still miss her."

Lizzie nodded, and her chin nudged Willow's breast-
bone. "But I don't miss her as much," she murmured
on a hiccup, "since you came to Summerhill. I'm sorry,
Willow, that I've been so difficult. I've been really
mean to you 'cos I was trying not to like you."

"That's all right, sweetie. I think you were testing
me, to see if I would be like the others and leave, or if
you could trust me to stay."

Lizzie looked up and Willow saw that her eyes were
heavy, her smile sleepy. "I do trust you to stay,

Willow.'' She yawned, and her eyelids started to drift shut. ''I know now that you *are* going to stay. Forever.''

Tears suddenly blurring her eyes, Willow scooped the child up in her arms and carried her through to her bed. By the time she reached it, Lizzie was sound asleep.

After tucking her in, Willow returned to the bathroom, and locked herself in. She stayed there, distraughtly pacing the small room, back and forth as she tried unsuccessfully to hold back her tears.

She wouldn't be staying at Summerhill forever. There was no doubt that she had enraged Lizzie's father with her exuberant exhibition on the dance floor.

Before this night ended, she knew that he would be sending her packing, and once again Lizzie and Mikey and Amy would be left swinging in the breeze.

By the time Camryn came looking for her to tell her the party was over, Willow was sitting quietly in Amy's darkened room…and had earlier sponged her eyes with cold water so often there was no sign that she'd been weeping, and she had—at least on the surface—become calm.

She felt totally washed out, though, and exhausted; and she prayed that Scott wouldn't try to make conversation on the way home. He didn't. He did usher her into the front seat, though, after escorting her to the car, but he could hardly have done otherwise. And she could hardly say to him that she'd rather be in the back, alone.

So they traveled home in silence. Not a companionable silence, a silence that throbbed with tension.

She fully expected that when they reached Summerhill, he'd turn on her, tear a strip off her. So she braced herself for a tirade after he switched off the engine…but

when he spoke, he didn't seem angry. He seemed...
withdrawn.

"You must be tired." He didn't look at her, she could
see the outline of his profile as he stared ahead into the
dark. "It's been a long night."

"Yes," she said. "Before I go in, though, Dr. Galbraith, I have to apologize for—"

He interrupted wearily, "I don't know what you think
you've done now, but for heaven's sake, stop saying
you're sorry—"

"The dancing, I know I shouldn't, I know it was out
of place, I know you were furious with me, I know I
should have stayed in the background, I know I've let
you down badly on every front, you wanted a plain-
Jane nanny, you made that clear from day one, a nanny
who'd blend into the woodwork—"

He jerked around in his seat and faced her; she
couldn't see his expression in the shadowy dark, but
she sensed it was grimly set—and there was no mistaking the intense frustration in his voice. "*You aren't
blendable!* Will you get that through your head, once
and for all? You're the very opposite of being blendable, dammit. You're a standout!" She saw a flash of
gold from his cuff links as he raked a hand through the
glossy strands of his jet-black hair. He hissed something
under his breath. It sounded like a curse. "We need to
talk!"

It was even worse than she'd thought. He was absolutely livid. She felt as if her stomach had become a
leaden lump—a lump that was as heavy as her heart.
This was it then. He was going to fire her.

Gathering up every shred of poise that she possessed,
and it certainly didn't amount to much, she said,
"About what, Dr. Galbraith?" As if she didn't know!

"For God's sake, will you stop calling me Dr. Galbraith? If I'm going to marry you, woman, you're going to have to start calling me Scott!"

CHAPTER ELEVEN

WILLOW had bungee-jumped. Once. And though tumbling down in free fall had absolutely terrified her, it had also charged her with a feeling of incredible joy.

She felt the same kind of joy now, a crazy wild joy that made her head spin.

But within moments her brain started to clear, and as she recalled that this was a man who had proposed marriage to someone else just a few scant hours earlier, she came down to earth with a sickening thud.

Camryn must have turned him down. And of course that had shattered him. But he hadn't taken long to recover...no *sirree!* If he couldn't marry for love, then he'd marry for convenience—and what could be more convenient than marrying the family nanny!

She felt a welling-up of fury and resentment. And afraid of what she might say to him if she opened the floodgates of her wrath and contempt, instead she got out of the car quickly and half walked, half ran toward the house.

Scott Galbraith was cold, calculating and selfish—an opportunist with his eyes fixed ruthlessly on the main chance.

And his main chance, now, was her.

Oh, she *despised* him!

She leaped up the steps to the front door, and was extricating her key from her purse, when she heard his heavy steps on the gravel and then he was pounding up the steps behind her.

Grabbing her by the shoulders, he spun her to face him.

In the unforgiving beam from the lamp above, she could see his expression. She thought it seemed anguished. Anguished? Huh! A trick of the light. It *must* be. What did he have to look anguished about? Certainly not because she'd fled from him. If he was anguished, it was because Camryn had rejected his proposal and broken his heart.

And that thought—the thought of his broken heart— blunted the sharp edges of Willow's rage. Oh, not enough that she didn't want to make him *grovel*. She still did!

And she planned to do it in such a subtle way he wouldn't even see it coming.

"Was that—" she flicked up an eyebrow "—a proposal?"

"Yes." He nodded vehemently. "It was. A proposal of marriage. Willow—"

"And when, exactly, did you decide to make this offer?"

She saw his Adam's apple bob up and down, and as she awaited his response she took a certain grim pleasure in his obvious agitation.

"I, um, actually, earlier this evening. Willow…let me explain—"

"And why, exactly, did you decide to propose to me?" She tilted her head to one side and regarded him with a little smile. "Am I to understand," she asked with deceptive softness, "that…earlier this evening… you suddenly discovered you were in love with me?"

"Dammit, yes! Madly in love, hopelessly in love—"

"And would that discovery—" she set a fist on one

hip and challenged him with a scornful glare "—have been before, or after, you proposed marriage to your sister-in-law?"

He gaped at her, his eyes abulge, his mouth wide-open.

He resembled, mused Willow, a fish out of water— one that had been stranded on a sandy beach under a blazing tropical sun without a tree or a sheltering bush in sight.

She felt not one scrap of pity for him.

"Before," she repeated her question relentlessly, "or after?"

"What...?" he choked out. "How...? I don't...I didn't...I'm not...she wouldn't...we're not...we weren't... I can explain—"

"Oh, *pullease!*" Rolling her eyes, Willow slipped her key into the lock. "Spare me the details."

She shoved the door open and stepped regally into the hall. Over her shoulder as she stalked across the foyer to the stairs, she called back, "Even if I were in love with you, which I am not, I wouldn't marry you for all the gold in all the banks in the world. I may be just a small-town girl with a small-time job and a small-time life, but I've never played second fiddle to anyone and I certainly have no intention of starting now!"

Behind her, the door crashed shut. She heard his steps as he came after her. With a feeling of panic, she made for the stairs and ascended them with deerlike speed.

When she reached the landing she hurtled on toward her room, bolted headlong inside and slammed the door.

Scott skidded to a halt, just in time to hear the lock click into place.

Dammit, she was *determined* to avoid him.

But he was just as determined not to go to bed till he'd had this out with her. He had to explain…

He *knew* she was in love with him…or at least, she had been till he'd doused the flame when he'd turned her off by pretending to be arrogant and full of himself. But once he'd cleared that up, surely she would tumble right back into love with him again? He prayed it would be so.

He knocked again. ''Willow…I'm not going to go away. If necessary, I'll kick the door in.''

No answer.

He turned and leaning his back against the locked door, stared down at his polished black shoes. ''Just listen,'' he pleaded. ''I have three things to say to you and once I've said them, if you want me to go, I'll go. But…just hear me out.''

The door opened suddenly and he lost his balance and almost fell backward. Staggering upright, he grabbed the doorjamb for a moment to steady himself, before swiveling around to face her.

She stepped back but kept her cold gaze fixed on him.

''All right.'' Her voice was thin and even colder than her wintry-gray eyes. ''But nothing you can say is going to make any difference to how I feel about you.''

''First of all,'' he said quickly, ''after Amy spilled the beans about your having told your mother you were falling in love with me—'' he saw dull burgundy color seep into her cheeks ''—and I made all those cutting remarks about not being surprised and about being used to females going gaga over me because I was—''

''God's gift to women,'' she snapped. ''Don't remind me. It's not something I care to remember. Of all the male chauvinists I've ever met, you are—''

''I faked it.'' He took a step toward her, she took two

steps back. He halted. "Willow, I *don't* think I'm God's gift to women…far from it. In fact, I'm a dead loss where women are concerned—I haven't a clue how their minds work—they're an absolute mystery to me! Not only that, I forget birthdays, and I forget anniversaries—"

"And when you look in the mirror every morning—" her upper lip curled in something close to a sneer "—you don't see the most attractive man within a thousand miles?"

"No, I damn well do not. I see a man who's doing his best to stumble through life, after losing his wife. A man who's trying his best to bring up their three children—and was making a sorry mess of it till you came along. I see a man who fell in love again when he least expected to—"

"With Camryn, of course." The wine-dark flush had seeped from her cheeks, leaving them pale as champagne. She had clasped her hands around her elbows, and despite the warmth in the room, she looked as if she were chilled to the marrow. "But she turned you down."

The defeat in her bearing gave him hope. Just a shred of hope that perhaps he still had a chance with her, but enough to propel him on. "Which brings me to my second point. Yes, I did propose to Camryn and yes, she did turn me down."

He saw a sparkle in her eyes. Tears? Oh, Lord, he hoped so. "And that—" he inhaled a deep breath and went on softly "—is why I'm here."

"Second fiddle…"

He took two steps forward. She took three steps back and came up against the edge of the bed. She could go no farther. He took four steps forward and took her in his arms. "Never second fiddle!" She was trembling, but when she tried to pull away, he just held her tighter. "I'm not in love with Camryn and she's not in love with me. But she did tell me something I'd been denying to myself for the longest time—which brings me nicely to my third point. I'm firing you from your post as nanny—"

She stiffened. But before she could try again to pull herself free, he said, tenderly, "Because the woman I'm in love with is you, and I want you to be, not the family nanny, but…my wife."

Her eyes had become dazed. "I don't understand. Why did you propose to Camryn if—"

"If I'm not in love with her?" His laugh was wry. "Because marrying my sister-in-law seemed like a perfect plan. I've known her for years, we'd always been good friends, we enjoy the same things, the kids love her, she loves the kids—"

"But why did she turn you down?"

"She said that like me, she'd thought in the beginning that it would be a perfect plan, an ideal partnership. But last night, before I even proposed to her, she'd changed her mind. She had decided a marriage of convenience—which is what it would have been—was not for her. She'd decided to wait for the right man…a man who would look at her the way she saw me looking at you while you were dancing…as if I loved you more than life itself."

"Oh." The sound was barely a whisper. "I saw you looking…and you seemed so…intense…I thought you were…angry with me."

"I was jealous. Bile-green with jealousy! But at the time, I didn't recognize the feeling. It wasn't one I was familiar with! And I was still struggling to deny that

what I felt for you was more than just physical desire.
I panicked. I took off, and when Camryn came after
me, I didn't waste any time in proposing. And that's
when she told me what she'd seen in my face as I'd
watched you, and I knew I couldn't deny it any longer.''

She was crying now. A tear rolled over her lower
eyelid and trickled down the side of her nose. With a
gentle fingertip, he caressed it away. "Oh, Willow, my
love, you will marry me, won't you, and put me out of
my misery?''

As she lay in bed that night, Willow choked back sob
after sob, her heated cheek pressed to a pillow that was
wet with tears. She loved Scott desperately but she
couldn't marry him. And she could hardly bear to remember the look on his face when she'd told him so.

"But why?" he'd cried.

She hadn't been able to answer. Not at first. But finally, when she'd gathered herself together sufficiently
to get the words out, she'd said, "I just can't. And I'm
sorry, the reason is…private.''

"Is it me? You don't love me? I was wrong…Amy
was wrong, you didn't tell your mother you were falling
for—''

"I did," she said, her voice thick with unhappiness.
"I did tell Mom I was falling in love with you.''

"Then why won't you marry me? Do you still think
me selfish and chauvinistic and conceited and—''

"No, no, no! I think you're wonderful.''

"But you won't marry me.''

She'd shaken her head. "I can't.''

He'd framed her face in his hands then, tightly, so
she couldn't move. "Willow, you have to tell me why.''

"It…it's got to do with Jamie." She'd choked out

the words. "About his...father. I'm sorry, I can't say anymore. I won't, but believe me, if you knew the story, knew how I've deceived you, you wouldn't want me anyway."

He must have seen, in her face, or heard, in her voice, that she was not going to change her mind.

So in the end, with his expression grimly set, he'd wheeled away and walked out of the room.

She'd thrown herself onto the bed and cried her eyes out. If only, she thought despairingly, if only she and Chad had never met. If only she hadn't written him that letter, telling him she no longer loved him and didn't want to see him anymore.

She was the one responsible for his death.

She had delivered the letter to Summerhill—had actually given it into the hands of Scott himself, though she hadn't known his identity at the time. And later, when Chad had read what she'd written, he'd been so heartbroken he'd jumped off the Camden Tower.

It had been cowardly of her to write him a Dear John letter; she would never forgive herself for that. If she'd given him the news face-to-face, she would have been there to talk to him, to calm him down, to reassure him that he would eventually fall in love again.

But she hadn't been there for him, and she *had* been a coward. And she was sentenced to have that on her conscience for the remainder of her days.

And she knew that if Scott ever found out she was responsible for the death of his stepbrother, he would never be able to look at her without thinking of it.

And because she had deceived him so outrageously, he would despise her as much as she despised herself.

She had to leave Summerhill.

She couldn't possibly stay on, after what had happened this evening. It would tear her apart to leave the children and she knew it would hurt them enormously.

But what alternative did she have?

Scott woke up next morning with a blinding headache—a headache that intensified when he recalled what had transpired the evening before.

Growly as a bear, he got out of bed and looked blearily around. The place was a mess: clothes everywhere, lying on the carpet where they'd landed after he'd ripped them off.

Moving around the room, he swept up his shirt, his tie, his pants. As he picked up his blazer, an envelope slid out of the inside breast pocket and fell to the floor.

He picked it up and looked at it blankly. He knew nobody had given him a letter last night. How long had this one been in that pocket? Curiosity stirring, he turned it over. And saw, printed neatly, his stepbrother's name.

He blinked. The letter was for *Chad?* How odd.

It must have been lying in his pocket since the last time he wore the jacket...which was seven years ago.

But how had he come to have it? Why had it been in *his* pocket? Who could possibly have—

Aah.

He nodded his head slowly as a vague memory started to stir. A memory of a summer night...seven years ago...he'd come to Summerhill on a short visit to his parents.

He'd been in the kitchen alone, after dinner, when the back doorbell had rung. He'd gone to answer it, and someone—a young girl who'd skulked in the shadows—had thrust a letter at him and asked him to give it to Chad. He'd said ''Sure.'' But before he could add,

"He's out at the moment, I'll give it to him when he gets home," she'd taken off into the darkness.

He'd stuck the letter in his pocket, intending to give it to Chad when he turned up later. But Chad hadn't turned up. The next person to arrive at Summerhill had been the local police chief, who had arrived just before midnight to inform the family of Chad's tragic death.

Frowning now as he became swamped in painful memories, Scott fingered the envelope, turning it over and over. Chad was gone. This letter, whomever it was from, had never been delivered, had never been answered.

Should he open it, see what it said?

Or should he toss it, unread, into the garbage?

"You're looking tired this morning." The housekeeper took a batch of chocolate chip cookies from the oven as Willow drank the last drops from her mug of black coffee. "Are you *sure* I can't fix you a nice cooked breakfast?"

Willow shook her head. "Thanks, Mrs. Caird, but I'm not hungry."

"Overate at the dinner last night, did you?"

"Maybe I did," Willow murmured, but she knew she had not. She'd been so painfully aware of the man sitting next to her, the man she so desperately loved, that she'd hardly eaten a thing. And now...she dreaded seeing him again. "Where's Dr. Galbraith?"

"His mother-in-law phoned earlier—apparently the children were all restless and wanted to come home, so he's gone to collect them. He should be back soon."

Willow's heart gave a quick leap. She had already stuffed her belongings into her backpack and had come downstairs, expecting to have to face him. But now, if she hurried, she could leave without seeing him. It was the cowardly way, of course, but then she was a coward. That was something she had always known.

And he wouldn't really be surprised, when he came home and found her gone. He would understand that after what had transpired between them last night, it would be impossible for her to remain in his employ.

She started toward the door. "Thanks for the coffee, Mrs. Caird. I'm going to—"

"Oh, just a second, Willow."

Stifling an impatient exclamation, Willow said, "Yes?"

"The first time we met I said Daniel had talked about you, but I couldn't remember what it was he said. It came back to me this morning."

Willow's stomach muscles clenched. After Daniel had returned to Toronto, she'd thought she was safe. But now...

"It did?" She tried to sound casually interested, while all the time her nerves were screaming.

"It was about your dancing. He'd gone to a show the school had put on—*Grease*, I think it was—and you had the lead part. He raved on for days about how outstanding you were—" The housekeeper broke off, frowning. "Willow, you do look so *white* this morning! Why don't you go upstairs and lie down for half an hour? Take a break before the children come roaring in—you'll need it!"

Heady with relief that Daniel hadn't given her secret away, hadn't told his foster mother that she and Chad had been lovers, Willow actually managed a pale smile. "Thanks, Mrs. C. Yes, I think I will go upstairs now."

But not to lie down. Instead she would gather up her

backpack and using the front door, she would sneak away from Summerhill, like a thief in the night.

Like the coward that she was.

On reaching her bedroom, she hurried over to close the window before leaving. As she curled her fingers around the handle, she heard the sound of an approaching car.

And froze at sight of the familiar green car skimming fast up the driveway.

He was back.

She was too late.

Dismayed, she watched the vehicle pull to a halt on the graveled forecourt. Seconds later, the doctor and his children emerged from the car, and Willow's dismay intensified when he ushered them toward the front door.

Blocking her means of escape.

She would have to hang around up here till the coast was clear.

In the meantime, she knew that this bittersweet moment, this bittersweet image, would remain with her forever. She stared yearningly at this wonderful family who would never be *her* family. Mikey, so adorable. Amy, so sweet. Lizzie, so loyal. And their father, so strong, so kind, so loving. So *honest*.

If only...if only...

She swallowed the huge lump that had formed in her throat.

Suddenly Mikey took off toward the side of the house, to the path that led around to the back. "Willow!" he shouted. "I'm going to find Willow!"

His father called after him, "Hey, Mikey, we're going in the front!" but the child kept right on going.

"C'mon, kids." Scott's voice drifted up to Willow. "We'll go in by the kitchen door, too."

* * *

"Willow's upstairs," Mrs. Caird said to the children, as they sat at the kitchen table, munching on chocolate chip cookies. "I told her to go and have a lie-down—she wasn't looking well at all. Not used to the late night, I expect," she added, pouring a mug of coffee for her employer. "It might have been a bit too much for her."

Scott said, "Thanks," as he took the coffee. He was glad the nanny wasn't around. He hadn't been looking forward to seeing her again. He'd given the situation a lot of thought since last night, and he still wasn't sure how to handle it. How could he continue living in the same house with her, feeling the way he did now? It would be impossible. If only he knew what her secret was, but it was obvious she never meant him to find out and, therefore, they had reached a permanent impasse.

"Mrs. Caird," he said. "I'm going through to my study for a minute and then I have to go to the clinic and catch up on some paperwork. Could you keep an eye on these three till Willow comes downstairs?"

"Of course."

"Thanks, I appreciate it. Be good, kids."

"We will, Dad!"

Mug in hand, he left the kitchen and walked along the corridor to the front hall. As he crossed the hall, he heard a voice come from the stairwell.

"Dr. Galbraith—"

He jerked his head up and he saw the nanny coming slowly down the stairs. His heart missed a beat, as it did every time he saw her—and he felt a stab of concern when he saw how dark and enormous her eyes looked in her parchment-pale face. She was wearing a white T-shirt and black jeans, and carrying a bulging backpack in one hand. "Yes?" Worry about her gave his voice a sharp edge and he sounded curt.

She paused for a second and then resumed her slow descent, trailing her backpack behind her so it landed with a bump on each step. "I...want to talk to you." She sounded as if she were on the verge of tears.

In a gentler tone, he said, "Sure. Come into my study. Can I get you a mug of coffee?"

She shook her head.

And followed him into the study.

He crossed to his desk and set his coffee mug down. When he turned around to face her, she was standing in the middle of the room. Her backpack was at her feet. He tried to ignore it, tried not to think of what it meant. He couldn't. She was leaving. She had taken the decision out of his hands. And she might as well have ripped out his heart.

"So," he said, dragging a hand through his hair, "you're going."

She nodded, and he thought her eyes misted with tears, but she blinked and the sheen disappeared. "I have something I...need to tell you first."

"Do you want to sit down?" He indicated one of a pair of leather armchairs by the hearth.

"I'd rather stand."

He perched his hip on the edge of his desk. "Okay. So...shoot then. I'm all ears."

"This...is going to be very difficult." She smiled. At least, her lips twisted, but her eyes told a different story. They were filled with sadness. "You see, I'm a coward, and...if I hadn't been...I would have told you this a long time ago, and I should have. And if I hadn't, which I didn't, I should never have come to work at Summerhill—"

"Does this go back to last night? When you said you had a secret...concerning your son?"

She bit her lip, and then nodded.

"And...you're going to tell me now? But why? What's changed since last night? Why is it okay to tell me this morning?" There was a tension in the air that hadn't been there before; simmering, escalating. She'd told him he would despise her if he knew her secret. Was it possible that she was right? He felt as if he were balancing on a tightrope strung precariously between two high-rises. With no net to catch him if he fell.

She said, with a tremor in her voice, "I'm telling you because when I saw you and the children come home just now, as I watched you from my bedroom window...you and your family...I knew that you had a right to know the truth, and I had no right to keep it from you. Even though, for my own selfish reasons, I *desperately* wanted to."

"It's to do with *my* family?" Scott felt bewildered. "But...what secret could you possibly think you know about myself and the children? There *are* no secrets!"

He saw her throat muscles move convulsively, saw her clasp her hands tightly together at her waist.

"It's not about you and the children." Her voice was almost a whisper. "It's about...Chad."

CHAPTER TWELVE

"*CHAD?* I don't understand. What do you know about my stepbrother? You said I had the right to know the truth. What 'truth' can you possibly be talking about?"

Willow knew that if she didn't tell him now, she never would. She could feel trepidation sucking away her courage.

Grabbing on to every last scrap of grit she possessed, and feeling as recklessly self-destructive as a kamikaze pilot, she said on a quaver, "Chad and I...had an affair."

"*Chad?* And *you?*" He was looking at her with an expression of stunned disbelief.

She nodded. And added, unsteadily, with a feeling of desperation, "Jamie is Chad's son."

Now he looked as if she'd just fired a gun point-blank at his head. "Jamie is *Chad's* son?" His electric-blue eyes had widened, his expression had become dumbfounded. "You're telling me your little boy is... a...*Galbraith?*"

Numbly Willow nodded. And felt her muscles knot, her nerves judder, as she prepared for the stormy outburst ahead. She'd realized, years too late, that she'd had no right to keep the truth from Jamie's family, especially from Chad's mother. And now she would have to bear the consequences.

"Good God, Willow!" He threw out his hands in a bewildered gesture. "*This* is the secret you thought would keep us apart? On the contrary, the fact that your son is a Galbraith would—or should—have only brought us closer together!''

''That's not all—''

''Willow, dearest Willow, what kind of a man do you think I am that I would condemn you for having a teenage affair—'' As he spoke he moved toward her, reaching out to her, his intent obvious.

She stopped him with swiftly raised palms.

''Don't,'' she said hoarsely. ''There's…more—''

''Sweetheart, there's nothing you can tell me that—''

''Please.'' Her mouth felt lined with dry sand. But she had to go on. ''I haven't told you the…awful…part yet. And it's not going to be easy to talk about it, about what happened…so please…don't interrupt. If you do, I may not manage to finish.''

''Go ahead,'' he said softly. ''I won't interrupt. I promise. Just tell me everything…from the beginning.''

Willow didn't really know how she'd managed to get this far; would she be able to finish what she'd started? All she could do was pray that she would. To get it off her conscience, once and for all.

''Chad and I met when I was sixteen, he was two years older. We were attracted to each other, and we dated—secretly because he said his mother was a snob and wouldn't approve of us going out together. He swore he was in love with me and I…thought I was in love with him. I'd…never had a real boyfriend before.'' Unclasping her hands nervously, she walked over to the tall window, and stood with her back to the room.

''We spent that summer together, late in the evenings, whenever we could, but as I got to know him…well, he started to change. He became very moody. Unpredictable. He…started to frighten me.''

Her voice cracked. "Twice, I tried to break off our relationship, but both times there was a big scene and he *begged* me to give him another chance, he swore he'd kill himself if I left him. And then he'd be so sweet and caring for a while and I'd...fall for him again. But at the end of the summer, he became sullen and withdrawn and unkind...he was making me really unhappy and I realized I wasn't in love with him anymore."

Outside, a blue jay swooped past, a flash of lapis in the summer sun. "I decided then," she said shakily, "to break it off but I wanted to avoid a scene like before so instead of telling him to his face I...took the coward's way out. I wrote him a letter. You probably don't even remember, but you were here on a visit and you're the one I gave it to, that evening, to deliver. And—" she closed her eyes as the horror of that night returned to her "—when Chad read it he climbed up the Marsden Tower and...jumped off."

She heard a sharp hiss from behind her. An appalled hiss. And she could imagine the expression on his face, the shock he was feeling now that he knew about the awful way she'd behaved. Swallowing hard, she went on miserably, "So you see, I was responsible for Chad's death, and I can never forgive myself for that—nor could I expect *you* to."

The tension in the room was so thick it made her want to scream. What was he thinking? Why was he so quiet? Why wasn't he lashing out at her?

And why was she still standing with her back to him? Screwing up the tattered remnants of her courage, she turned to face him, bracing herself in expectation of his contempt.

She looked around—and blinked with surprise.

The room was empty.

He was gone.

Her life had never felt blacker, her heart never heavier. She had foolishly dared to hope—in view of his loving response when she'd revealed that Chad was Jamie's father—she'd actually dared to hope he might be equally loving and generous when he discovered her letter had driven Chad to his death.

It had obviously been far too much to expect. Why, the man couldn't even bear to stay in the same room with her—perhaps he'd left because he couldn't trust himself to keep his bitter emotions under control.

And he certainly wouldn't want to see her again.

Fighting back tears of self-pity, she wearily dragged her backpack from the carpet and slinging a strap over her shoulder, trudged mournfully from the room.

Upstairs, she could hear heavy steps moving around.

From the kitchen, she could hear the children laughing.

Wondering if she'd ever been unhappier in her life, she walked toward the front door—but halted suddenly when she was only halfway there.

She'd fully intended to sneak away without saying goodbye to Mikey and the girls. She dug her teeth into her lower lip so hard she winced. No, she was *not* going to sneak away. She was *never* going to be a coward again.

It would be agonizingly difficult to face the children and see their faces crumple with disappointment and betrayal when she told them she was leaving. But someone had to tell them, and she should be the one.

Like a robot, she turned and started toward the kitchen.

She'd taken only five steps when heavy steps pounded on the stairs.

"Willow!" Scott's tone was harsh. Demanding. "Where are you going?"

She turned and saw him leap down the last few steps and come striding over to her.

"Don't worry," she said quietly. "I'm leaving. But it's *my* place to tell the children I'm deserting them, no matter how difficult it's going to be. It's important that they hear it from me because—"

He held out an envelope.

"Is this the letter?" he asked.

For a moment all she could do was stare at it. What letter? And then, with a sickening lurch of her stomach, she recognized the pink envelope, with its deckle-edged trim. It was the notepaper she had used seven years ago; the notepaper she still used. And as she gazed at it, her stomach lurched again when she recognized her own black printing on the front. The printing that read: Chad.

"Where…did you find it?" Her voice sounded strangulated. "How long have you had it? When did you read it? How long have you known—"

He laughed, and the free and easy sound grated on her ears. How could he laugh when the situation was so unbearably tragic.

"I haven't read it, sweetheart."

He…was calling her "sweetheart"? Despite what she'd told him? Despite what she'd done? She couldn't wrap her mind around what was happening.

"I…I don't understand." She felt dizzy. Faint. "You haven't read it?"

His laughing expression faded and his eyes became serious. "Willow, nobody has *ever* read this letter. When you gave it to me that night, I stuck it in my pocket, meaning to give it to Chad when he came home…he was out when you called. But later, well, he didn't come home, it was the police who turned up. And with everything that followed, the letter slipped my mind. It's been lying in my blazer pocket—unopened— for the past seven years. It didn't come to my notice till this morning. And when I saw it, I decided to toss it, unread, into the garbage can in my bedroom. Which is where I retrieved it from just now!''

Willow swayed and he swiftly closed the space between them and took her in his arms. ''You weren't responsible for Chad's death, my darling. You had nothing to do with it!''

Willow's mind felt socked in by fog. And her voice came out foggily when she spoke. ''Let me see it, let me see the envelope.''

She took it from him and as she turned it over and saw that yes, it was still *sealed*, incredulity soared through her, making her feel as if she were dreaming. She looked up into Scott's eyes, and wondrous relief made her own eyes glisten with tears. ''You really didn't manage to give Chad my letter? You mean he never saw it, never read it—''

''Never knew, Willow, that he had lost your love.''

''But, I don't understand. I thought you said once that your father hushed things up so people would believe Chad had tripped, that his death was an accident. If he didn't jump then surely it *must* have been an accident.''

''It wasn't an accident.'' Scott knew that after her years of being tormented by guilt, she deserved to know the family's closely guarded secret. ''You said Chad had changed, and he had. The reason was that during that summer, he'd started dabbling in drugs. And he was high when—despite a friend's attempts to stop him— he stepped off the Marsden Tower believing he could fly.''

"Oh, no!" Horror-stricken, Willow could only stare at him. "How awful," she whispered, a sob in her voice. "How sad. Oh, poor Chad…" She started to cry, and as she did, Scott took her in his arms.

He let her weep, while he held her and murmured tender words of comfort, knowing that was all he could do for her; she had to come to terms with the truth but she would also find peace, knowing she'd not been to blame in Chad's death.

When she finally raised her head, she said, shakily, "Daniel Firth was the friend who was with Chad. Dan used to cover for Chad when we were out together…you noticed how seeing Dan distressed me…it was because I was afraid he'd find out I had a six-year-old son and he'd guess it must be Chad's."

"Obviously he never did. But now you needn't worry about that. Everybody's going to find out soon enough. As long as you don't mind."

"I'll be happy to have no more secrets to hide! How can I ever thank you for finding the letter, for taking away all my fears. I always felt so painfully guilty over Chad's death."

"You're not the only one." Scott touched his fingertips gently to her hair, caressing back a tendril that had wisped over her brow. "I always felt that if I'd come home more often, if I'd spent more time with Chad, things might have been different. But there's no changing the past, we must put it behind us. Only one more question before we do, Willow…"

"What is it?"

"You must have known what it would mean to Chad's mother to know she had a grandson. Chad told you she was a snob, but did you really think she'd have turned her back on Jamie?"

"No, the very opposite. I was afraid that if your family knew about my baby, they would try to take him away from me…and I couldn't take that risk."

"Willow, that would never have happened. I, for one, would never have allowed it to happen. Do you believe that?"

"I believe it now because I know you. But I didn't know you then…I didn't know what a kind and compassionate man you are. All I knew then was that the Galbraiths were rich and influential, and I was sure I wouldn't have had a chance against them in court if they fought me for custody."

"Chad's mother has been a changed woman since his death. She'll welcome you into the family, as warmly as she'll welcome Jamie. And now," he said, "we'll put the past truly behind us, and look to the future. There are two things I want you to do. The first—you must stop calling me Dr. Galbraith!"

She blushed. "It's not going to be easy."

"Try."

She wrinkled her dear little nose. "Scott…?"

"Oh, Willow!" He held her even closer. "I love you so much. What a fool I was, wasting all that time courting Camryn!"

"But you had a plan!" She was teasing him, and he was delighted to see the same spark in her eyes that he'd first seen the day they met in Morganti's. "A *Perfect* Plan!"

"A Perfect Plan indeed, and one I was hell-bent on carrying out. But I hadn't counted on the charms of a certain plain-Jane nanny who was far from plain and stole my heart…even as she healed the wounded hearts of my children."

"You said there were two things I had to do."
Willow tilted her head shyly. "What was the second?"

"The second is...you must marry me!"

"Oh, Scott, I can't think of anything I'd rather do!"
Willow beamed at him. "Won't it be fun, bringing up
our four children together?"

He framed her face in his hands. And with a smile
that made her heart sing, he whispered, in that brown
velvet voice she now loved so much,

"Who said anything about stopping at four!"

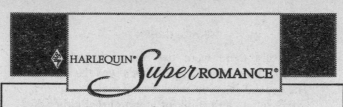

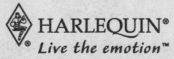

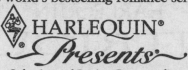

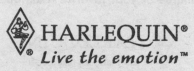